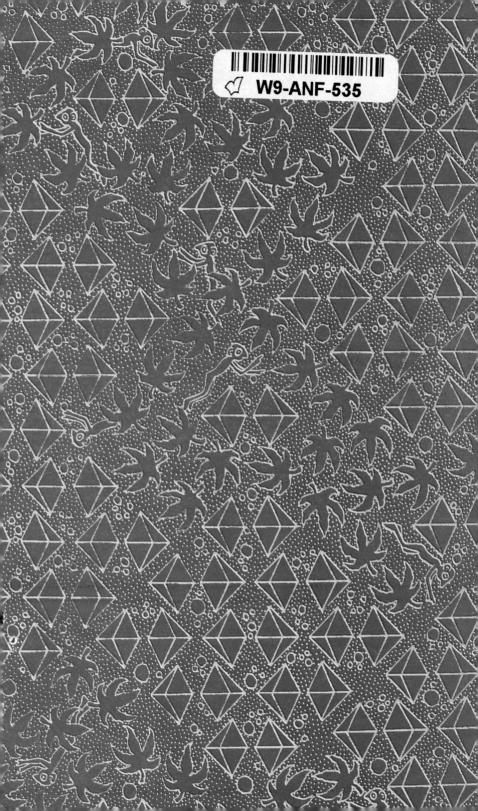

the magic
spectacles

THE MAGIC SPECTACLES

by
James P. Blaylock

illustrated by Ferret

MORRIGAN PUBLICATIONS
1991

published by
MORRIGAN PUBLICATIONS
84 IVY AVENUE
BATH AVON BA2 1AN

Of this first edition, 260 copies include an additional
postscript by Lewis Shiner. Of these; 250 are
specially bound, slipcased and signed; and 10 copies are
bound in leather and are for presentation purposes only.

TRADE EDITION ISBN 1 870338 95 2
SPECIAL EDITION ISBN 1 870338 01 4

Typeset and printed by
The Longdunn Press Ltd, Barton Manor, St. Philips,
Bristol, BS2 0RL.

To *Viki*

And to the Eckes family,
Kimberly, Michael, Lynn and *Tom*

CHAPTER ONE

PANCAKES AND AUTUMN LEAVES

A curiosity shop appeared in the centre of a row of small stores near the Plaza. That is to say, it hadn't seemed to be there yesterday, and it was a shop that sold curious things. If you stood across the street you couldn't quite say what it sold. The window wasn't so much dirty as it was misty. It seemed cobwebby, but it wasn't that either.

Wooden strips criss-crossed the windows, which might have made them a little harder to see through. And bending over the street in front of the shop were two great camphor trees, shaking lime-green leaves in the breeze. It was almost as if the trees were laughing, although what they might have been laughing at, you couldn't say. Maybe they laughed at the curious things in the window of the shop. Maybe they laughed at you and at your leafy reflection in the dusty glass.

The Plaza was a circle of grass and trees in the middle of downtown, in the city of Orange, where John and his brother Daniel lived. It had a fountain in the middle of it, the Plaza did, and some people said that the water in that fountain came from a long way under the ground, maybe from lakes in the centre of the earth. It was an almost magical place. Looming over the fountain was a big sycamore tree, very old, with four low branches that pointed toward the four points of the compass. It was the first tree to find its leaves in the spring, and the first to lose them again in the autumn.

7

The curiosity shop appeared one of those autumns, right after Halloween. During that particular season it seemed to John as if there was a lot of uneasiness in the air, like the shadow of something you couldn't see. The grass in the plaza turned brown, as if it were asleep, and the fountain itself got rusty and clogged for some reason. Half the time it wouldn't work at all, and the water was hazy with dirt.

The maple syrup at the lunch counter at Watson's Drug Store went sour almost as soon as it was opened, and so did the milk. But what was worse was that the sparrows that nested in and around the plaza started to disappear. Some of them were found lying on the grass, as if they had just given up, like the grass had, and gone to sleep; others flew away and didn't come back. Some said it was because the birds drank water from the fountain. Others said that there was something in the air.

People who worked around the Plaza began to fall asleep at the strangest times of day. Shopkeepers dozed in their chairs, and waiters took naps while their customers waited for hamburgers. Old Mrs. Jimson, on Grand Street, fell asleep in the rocker on her front porch and couldn't be awakened, although she seemed to be sleeping very naturally and peacefully.

Things began to disappear, too, mostly things made of glass. None of it was very valuable, except Dr. Stone's pocketwatch, which was later found in the parking lot of Higgin's Furniture Store. Someone had pried the lens off and then thrown away the watch. Glass costume jewelry was stolen from an antique store while the clerk slept with his head on the counter, and a box full of prisms from old lamps disappeared from Mr. Reese's Antique Barrel. Mr. Reese said that a little bitty man, like a goblin, had stolen the prisms right out from under his nose, and Dr. Stone said he believed it, because it was a little man who had got his pocketwatch.

One Friday afternoon, before the curiosity shop appeared, John and Daniel rode their bicycles down to the Plaza, where they sat on a bench and ate Halloween candy—licorice witches and candy-corn pumpkins. Across the street was a dark, empty store. It sat between a store that sold old

8

clothing and another that sold paint. The windows were covered with dust.

Someone had rubbed off a little circle of dust in order to see out, and, maybe, to let other people see in. Danny wanted to have a look, but John didn't. There was something about looking into the dark and empty store that John didn't like, although he couldn't say why. It was just a feeling that he had. But Danny said that he was going to have a look one way or another, and that John could sit on the bench across the street and wait, if he was scared of looking in. Danny waited for a break in the traffic and ran his bike across the crosswalk. At the window, he bent over and cupped his hands against the glass.

John watched him, wondering what his brother saw. It must be something good, because he was looking for a long time. Either that, or he was *pretending* it was something good. John wanted to see too. He didn't want Danny to be the only one to know. Danny was what people called the 'adventurous type.' He loved climbing over fences and onto roofs and checking out empty buildings to see what was going on. He was a little thin, although not skinny, and he had curly, light-brown hair that he didn't usually bother to comb, but which seemed to comb itself and always looked good. His eyes were brown that was speckled with green, and the green speckles made them twinkle, as if he was always up to something.

John was built bigger and had straight brown hair, which he didn't bother to comb either, because almost no matter what he did to it, it would fall straight down over his forehead anyway. He *wasn't* what people called the adventurous type, although he liked adventure well enough when it found him. He was the responsible, worrying type, and right now he was worried about messing around the old store when they had no business there. Nothing happened to his brother, though, as he stood looking into the window. No one came out and shouted at him or anything. "What is it?" John yelled.

Danny shrugged his shoulders, but he didn't turn around. He kept on looking. He was probably doing it on purpose, John thought, in order to *make* him come across.

Climbing onto his bicycle, John rode once around the fountain, as if he wasn't really in any hurry, and then he coasted down onto the crosswalk and across the street, skidding his bike up next to his brother's.

"Let me see," John said.

Danny stepped aside. "Sure," he said. "There's nothing to see."

And he was right. John couldn't really see anything but an old wooden floor and late afternoon shadows and the reflections of leaves. It was dark and murky inside the store. "I told you," he said.

"Told me what?" Danny asked.

"That there wasn't anything here."

Just then there was a noise from inside, like a scraping and moving of furniture. Something banged down onto the wooden floor, and then there was the sound of whistling, like someone working very hard and enjoying it.

John hopped onto his bicycle and took off, away from the Plaza toward Maple Street. It was a moment before he looked back to see if Danny was behind him. He wasn't. John stopped, almost a block from the empty store, to wait for his brother. He would go back after him in a moment, if he had to. Danny came around the corner just then, pedalling his bicycle as if he wasn't in any hurry. When he got close, John said, "Did you look back in? It sounded like ghosts working or something."

"Yes," said Danny. "There was still nothing in there. I knew there wouldn't be."

John wasn't so sure.

On Saturday morning, the next day, everything had changed.

They rode back down to eat pancakes at Watson's Drugstore and passed the empty shop on the way. Only it wasn't empty anymore. The windows were still dusty and shaded, but just beyond them now was a clutter of stuff.

John rode straight past it. He wasn't sure why. Danny stopped, but he didn't get off his bicycle. When John looked back and saw his brother looking at the stuff in the window, he stopped too, to wait. But then it seemed to him that he was *always* waiting while Danny found something out, and so although he was a little bit troubled about the place, he rode back down and pulled up next to his brother.

The window was full of curious things. John thought that he could just make out an elephant's foot made into a stand for holding umbrellas. Beside it was a stuffed crow and the skeleton of a big lizard with a red jewel in either eye. Piles of books tilted against each other, all of them dusty and old. There was a fishbowl full of marbles, too, and in the middle of the marbles, shoving up through them, was a pair of old spectacles with brass wire rims.

Beyond all this stuff was what looked like the picture of a little man in a pointed cloth night cap. But the man very suddenly disappeared, so he couldn't have been a picture after all. John edged away from the window. "Let's go," he said.

Just then a breeze blew up and the camphor trees on the curb rustled and danced. A great sheet of wrapping paper, all orange and red and yellow, whirled past on the wind, end over end like a pinwheel down the centre of the street. Behind it rushed a circus of dead autumn leaves, and the sky was filled with the screech of wild parrots and the cawing of crows. It was the first part of November.

The sycamore and maple and flowering pear trees had turned colour. And there was something on the wind— some smell—as if someone far away had made a bonfire of tree prunings and the breeze was full of smoke that you couldn't see.

Something in John wanted to have a look inside the curious shop, but not just yet. It wasn't exactly the day for it. Or maybe then again it was, and that's what troubled him. They walked down to the cafe at Watson's Drug Store and ordered pancakes and sausages and hot chocolate, as they did almost every Saturday morning.

John stacked his pancakes on top of each other and cut a hole in the centre of them about as big as a quarter. He dropped a little circle of butter into the hole and watched it melt into the hot pancakes. He wouldn't put a drop of syrup on them until the butter had disappeared, but then he would fill the hole with syrup and wait for it to soak in too. It was important to do it just right. Danny didn't stack his pancakes at all, or put syrup on them either. He spread them with peanut butter, rolled them up, and then ate them with his fingers. All the time they were there, sitting in front of the window messing with pancakes, they watched people hurry along on the sidewalk.

It wasn't awfully cold outside, but it was blustery. The wind made people clutch their coats around them as if it were going to blow them off and sail them over the rooftops like kites. A man raced past chasing a hat, and another man, right behind him, hurried along backwards so that the wind blew his coat shut instead of open.

Then a dry and scratchy palm frond blew against the window in a rush as if it were shouting something. It clattered to the sidewalk and lay still. The wind stopped blowing. Flying leaves drifted to the street. People let go of their coats and pulled the collars straight. John pushed his plate away. His cocoa was gone; there was nothing left in his cup but a sort of brown paste.

They'd eaten enough anyway. It was time to go. John took four crumpled dollar bills from his pocket, and Danny dug out a handful of change, mostly nickels and dimes. They counted out the coins, heaping them on top of the bills, making sure there was enough and with some left over for a tip. Out of the corner of his eye, John saw that someone was watching at the window.

It was a little man, smaller even than Danny, who was smaller than John. His face was wrinkled and pinched. He took a green cloth cap from the pocket of his coat and pulled it on. Then he winked at them, very slowly, screwing up his face awfully.

It was the little man that John had seen in the curiosity shop. And John knew, all of a sudden, that he had seen the man before then too. It had been over a month ago—right at the end of summer, in the week before school started. That's why he remembered it. He remembered everything about that week—how it had rained for two days and how he and Danny had floated paper boats in the gutter. There had been a lightning storm Friday night, and they had made their father build a fire in the fireplace even though it was really still summer and wasn't very cold at all.

12

Also, at the beginning of that week, the two of them had been playing baseball on the front lawn, though John knew they shouldn't be, and Danny had hit the ball through their bedroom window. There had been nothing left of the window but shattered glass all over the bedroom floor, and it had taken their mother half an hour to clean it all up.

Even the wooden frame of the window was wrecked—not from the baseball, but from being old and weathered and falling apart. Anyone could see that it wouldn't do just to put in another piece of glass. The window must be taken out and repaired, or else replaced altogether.

That's when they got lucky, and Mrs. Owlswick down the block gave them a window. It was just the right size, too. Mrs. Owlswick lived along with her niece Kimberly in a big and very old house. Under the house, in a little cellar, Mrs. Owlswick had a lot of odds and ends of stuff: pieces of lumber and a box of glass doorknobs and brass hinges, and of course the window, which was glazed with a curious, ripply sort of pale green glass.

This window, which Mrs. Owlswick gave to John and Daniel, was just the right size to replace the broken one in the boys' bedroom. In fact it seemed almost as if that was what Mrs. Owlswick's window had been built for in the first place.

Their father said that he was 'going to do the job right,' which usually meant he was going to do it in the most complicated way he could, and make the job last for days. He pulled off the wall mouldings and pried the old window out, rehanging the iron weights inside the wall with fresh cotton rope. "Good as new," he had said the next evening, when he was done. Then he had thrown the broken window into the trash, frame and all, and pounded the mouldings back up around Mrs. Owlswick's window.

Now, of course, it wasn't Mrs. Owlswick's window. It belonged to John and Danny. But it was peculiar to look through, and seemed to be very old with its wavy, green-coloured glass. It made the front porch look like a tidepool, as if you were gazing out through shallow sea water.

13

That was the week of the lightning storm. The morning after the lightning it had still been raining. John had been sitting on his bed, looking out through Mrs. Owlswick's window at the street. Water ran in the gutter, splashing over the curb, and windy raindrops splattered against the window.

While John had sat there watching, someone with an umbrella came along down the sidewalk. He was small, so John had thought he was a boy—maybe new in the neighbourhood. He was walking slowly, enjoying the weather. Rain poured off his umbrella in a curtain of drops, and he wore black rubber boots so he could splash through puddles as much as he liked and not get his pants wet. On his head was a green, pointed, cloth cap. He was a little man with a wrinkled face, and not a boy at all.

He had stood on the sidewalk twirling his umbrella for a moment, looking at the house—or more particularly, looking at the new window, maybe looking through it at John. On his back was a bundle of sticks, as if he were out collecting firewood. Abruptly he walked on, past Mrs. Owlswick's old house and off toward the north. John had stepped across to the window and watched him get smaller and smaller as he disappeared down the sidewalk. Two blocks down, well past Colin's house but not yet to the third corner, he vanished in the misty morning air.

All of that—the window, the storm, the little man with the umbrella—had happened a month ago. One other thing had happened too. The sky had cleared that afternoon, and the full moon shone overhead at mid-day. Their father told them that earthworms loved to play when the moon was out on a rainy day, so John and Danny had gone out to hunt up worms on the lawn in order to sail them in paper boats in the gutter. Straightaway, Danny had found a two-headed coin on the sidewalk, and had put it into his pocket as a good luck charm.

Now, a month later, here was the little man in the pointy green cap, looking in at them through the window of Watson's Drug Store. By the time John and Danny got outside, he had crossed the street and gone into the curiosity shop.

It was a strange business, as if something was in the air, something sad and still, something waiting. Of course it always seems as if there is something in the air when autumn comes. The ghost of Halloween is still on the wind, even in November, and so is the promise of Christmas, and then of lonesome, rainy days that are good for messing around in the garage. But on this particular Saturday morning there was something more.

They rode their bicycles across to the Plaza and sat around by the fountain, picking dead leaves out of the cold and murky water, which barely trickled now out of the pipes. John knew that Danny was thinking the same thing that he was—that he would like to have that fishbowl full of marbles in the window of the curiosity shop.

They each had some money left in their pockets, but to buy the marbles they would have to go into the shop. They would have to talk to the little man in the green hat, and the truth was that he made John feel uneasy, as did his curiosity shop. It had made him uneasy yesterday when it was empty, and it made him about twice as uneasy now that it was full. The little man must have worked through the night to get all that stuff in there. He looked like the kind of little man who could turn you into a bird or a toad or something, the sort of thing you might read about, in a story by G. Smithers, John and Danny's favourite writer.

But good marbles were hard to find. You could buy clear marbles in a plastic net bag at the market. And you could buy solid colour marbles like the ones that come in a Chinese checkers game. Cats' eyes were common enough; you found those sometimes in the dirt of a flowerbed, dropped there years ago by kids who are grown up now and don't care about marbles anymore.

But you couldn't find any of the old sorts of marbles, with rainbow spirals of colour and each one different than all the rest. Some were like swirls of frozen rootbeer, or reminded you of tigers, or of a sunlit forest; others looked like the earth seen from way off in space, as if you were sitting on the moon.

The fishbowl was full of those sorts of marbles—old, swirly marbles with deep, clear colours. John wanted to buy them all. Marbles were like any sort of treasure; you needed a pile of them. The bigger the pile the better.

They leaned their bikes against the brick wall of the building, stood back, and studied the shop front. A sign hung in the door. On it was painted a picture of an old man with a crutch and carrying a bundle of sticks. There was a full moon in the sky above him. Under the painting were the words, COME IN.

So they did.

CHAPTER TWO

THE FISHBOWL FULL OF MARBLES

It was dark and cool inside. The little man in the hat was nowhere to be seen. The shop was full of odds and ends, all of it dusty, piled on old tables and falling in heaps out of open wardrobes and spilling from the shelves of bookcases. To look at it, you would think it had been there for years.

Hanging from the rafters in the high ceiling was the skeleton of a giant bird held together with silver wire. There were books everywhere, all of them dark and old. There were piles of stuffed bats and pictures of apes and clipper ships and old houses and serious looking people in bonnets and top hats. There was a jar with an enormous eye in it, and no end of old candles and silverware and crystal glasses. On the counter there was a lamp built out of a great iron fish.

Suddenly, there was the little man himself, sitting behind the counter on a tall stool. He had a book in his hand, and he looked at John and Daniel over the top of it, sort of peeking at them. His cloth bag full of tied-together sticks lay on the floor in front of the counter. He must have been there all along, and they simply hadn't seen him behind the piles of stuff. "What do you need?" he asked them in a voice that sounded as if it came from a long way away, as if someone were shouting at them from the moon.

Danny stepped closer to John, and John said, "Nothing."

"Marbles," Danny said.

The little man watched them. They could only see his

17

eyes and half his nose. The rest of him was hidden by the book and the counter. "Nothing or marbles?" he said. "You can't want both, can you?"

"Marbles, then," said John.

Then Danny said, "In the fishbowl, we mean. In the window. We don't need the glasses, though."

The little man nodded. The point of his green cap wagged up and down. "You see very clearly, then, do you?"

John shrugged and kicked Danny's foot just to make sure that Danny knew how weird all this was. "I guess we just don't want the glasses. They're really very nice and all, but what we want are the marbles. As many as we can buy."

Danny dug the rest of the change out of his pocket, holding it out for the man to see. "We don't have very much," Danny said.

Slowly the man's head rose over the top of his book, until his whole face peered down at Danny's handful of pennies and nickels. He nodded his head slowly. "Do you have a penny with two heads on it?" he asked, rubbing the side of his nose.

John started to shake his head. Pennies, after all, had only one head, just like people. But then he remembered the rainy-day penny. Danny, having carried the two-headed coin in his pocket for over a month, as good luck, dug through the rest of his change. He turned the pennies over in his hand and put each one away into his pocket.

At last there was one coin left. It was very old, and had turned a little bit green, like moldy cheese. In the dim light, it was hard to see *what* was on it. Danny rubbed it. Then, looking first at John, he climbed up onto an empty wooden crate and held the penny under the light of the iron fish lamp so that you could see the face that was on the front and back both. John stepped up next to him in order to get a look at it.

On it was the face of a man who was maybe a little too fat. He was almost bald, too, and had only a sort of ring of hair above his ears. His eyes were shut, as if he were asleep. But just when John looked closely at the face, the eyes seemed to move behind their eyelids, as if in an instant they would open. John nearly fell over backward with the

18

surprise of it. Danny dropped the penny as if it were hot, and it clattered down onto the painted base of the lamp and lay there. The little man put his book down, and took out from under the counter a magnifying glass and a pair of long tweezers.

It was ghostly silent in the store. Outside, the wind blew once more. John could see the camphor trees dancing and people hurrying past, clutching their coats again. The Man put the glass to his eye. Then he plucked up the penny with the tweezers and turned it over slowly.

He looked up at them through the magnifying glass. His eye was enormous, like the eye of a whale. "This is just what I want," he said, nodding at them. "Two heads. These are very rare. You don't see one in a thousand years. I saw you eating pancakes this morning."

John nodded. The little man had a funny way of talking. His talk didn't seem to go in a straight line.

"Like pancakes, do you?"

Danny nodded now. There was almost nothing better than pancakes and peanut butter.

"It's *eating* I like," said the little man. "Better than anything. Take the marbles if you want them, but they aren't all there; there's one missing. They used to belong to a man, but he gave them all up except one." He picked up the penny with the tweezers and dropped it through a slot cut in the top of the iron fish. Several seconds later there was a clank and a rattle of coins, as if the penny had fallen a long long way, to the bottom of a well, maybe, and landed on top of a mountain of pennies.

"How many marbles can we buy?" John asked. "All together we have about eighty cents, I think."

"All of them," came the reply. "Didn't I say I wanted a penny with two heads? Didn't you give me one? Take all the marbles, and the spectacles too. And the fishbowl with them."

He picked up his book again and pretended to read. But John was pretty sure that he watched them over the top of the pages when they walked across and picked up the fishbowl and went out. The wind slammed the door shut with a bang behind them. The two of them jumped in

19

surprise, and when they turned around to look, it seemed to them that the interior of the shop was even darker than it had been. Way back in the shadows glowed the fish lamp, like a lonesome star in the night sky.

The sign hanging in the door had changed, as if it had been turned around. The old man painted on it was walking away from them now, the bundle of sticks thrown over his back. CLOSED UP, the sign read.

John set the fishbowl very carefully in his basket, since Danny's bike didn't have one. He did it quick, too. Somehow he felt as if he were in a terrible hurry. Danny acted the same way, climbing onto his bicycle and pedalling off down the sidewalk, around the corner and across the parking lot, then up and into the alley that would take them to Pine Street where their house was.

The wind blew into their faces, slowing them down. John stood up on the pedals and pushed harder, feeling as if he were in a dream, trying to run away from something but not being able to. It felt as if whatever he was running from was coming along with him, sitting right there in his bicycle basket. They swung off their bikes, running them up into the driveway and under the carport. In a moment they were inside, spilling the marbles out onto the rug in their bedroom, picking and choosing from among them, dividing the marbles into piles.

Both John and Danny had a special box, which they called a 'jewel box,' and they put the best of the marbles into their jewel boxes and snapped the latches. Each of them kept one of the best, though, to put into their pockets for good luck charms. John's was green and red, like a round piece of Christmas candy, and Danny's was pink and blue, the colour of an Easter egg.

They took the rest of the marbles outside, drew a ring in the dirt behind the swingset, and put ten of the marbles into the ring. Each of them had a shooter, and the point was to knock the marbles out of the ring with the shooter. John had learned the game at school.

It was hard going, though, in the bumpy dirt, especially for Danny, whose hands were smaller. The shooter kept spinning away into the bushes or in among avocado leaves,

and their dog, whose name was Ahab, kept shoving his nose into the circle full of marbles—which he suspected were really bugs—and snuffling them around.

After a little while, they heard the gate across the driveway scrape open. It was their friend Kimberly coming in. She was Mrs. Owlswick's niece and was the same age as John. She liked to play just about everything, including marbles, and when she found out that they had a whole fishbowl full of them she ran home to get some of her own, and then was back again in about a minute.

She had very long blond hair, which was tied into a pony tail with a red ribbon, and she was wearing a dress, because she was going out to lunch with her aunt. She only had a few minutes, she said. Her aunt, who had lived in the old house for a long long time, was very strict, or at least that's what John and Danny had heard. When they had met her, though, she seemed nice, and had given them cookies out of the freezer, which she called 'cold cookies'.

Kimberly's marbles were in a square red can with a hinged top. It had a picture on it of a house on a hill, above a meadow. The house had diamond-paned windows and smoke curling up out of three chimneys. Flowering vines grew across the porch, and on top of the roof a weather vane shaped like a fish pointed toward the rising sun, which was coming up between two hills. Under the picture were the words, 'East, West, Home's Best.'

"What a great can," said John. "Where did you get it?"

"It used to belong to my aunt," said Kimberly. "I found it with a lot of other stuff under the house, down where the window was."

"*You* found it under your house?" asked Danny.

"Yes," Kimberly said, taking aim at one of the marbles in the circle and shooting at it. There was a little cracking noise, as the two marbles hit, and then the marble from the circle rolled out. "Got it!" Kimberly shouted.

"What did you do," asked John, "just, like, climb under there or something? Weren't there spiders?"

Kimberly shook her head. She didn't seem to want to talk about it much. Maybe, thought John, because she had gotten into trouble for being under there. It was something that a very strict aunt might not like. She might think it was dangerous, what with all the lumber and windows and hardware and such down there.

"There weren't any spiders," said Kimberly, shooting again. "But there was this can, full of marbles, and a lot of old seashells and fishbones and some very pretty glass jewelry. Look."

She showed them, under her jacket, a jewelled star and a necklace of rhinestones and green glass.

John's eyes got very wide. "You found *those* under your house, too? It's like a whole treasure or something."

Kimberly nodded. "That's just what it was," she said. "A goblin treasure."

"Under your house?" asked Danny. "I never heard anything about goblins leaving treasure under a house."

"I never heard about them being under houses at all," John said.

Kimberly nodded at him. "They like living under houses well enough, when they have too. They'd rather live in the woods, of course, but sometimes they go out adventuring and have to make do with living under houses. But they're very sloppy with their treasures, leaving them lying around like that."

"Maybe that's the stuff that was taken from the shops near the Plaza," John said. "Maybe goblins took it and stashed it under your house."

"That's a lie!" said a voice, and all three of the children looked up to see Harvey Chickel standing there. "There's nothing under houses but dirt," he said. "I bet *she* stole it, and is making up stuff about goblins."

Kimberly looked straight at him and said, "Some people think that almost everything is just dirt. But they're wrong."

Harvey scowled at her. "They're not as wrong as you are," he said, and he looked for a moment like he was going to hit her. He had hit her at school once, and thrown his half-eaten ice cream bar at her, and had gotten into trouble for it. John hadn't been there, but when he had heard about it, it had made him mad. If he *had* been there, he would have given it to Harvey good. At least that's what he told himself. He wondered sometimes whether he *really* would

22

have, or whether he would have been too scared to. Maybe he would find out right now. Harvey seemed to want to start something, to cause trouble.

But just then there was someone calling on the sidewalk out front. It was Kimberly's aunt, Mrs. Owlswick. Kimberly picked up her can of marbles and ran off, and Harvey started to yell something after her, just to be able to say one more mean thing.

"Give it up," said John, but he didn't say it very loud. "Leave her alone, can't you?"

"Why?" asked Harvey, slumping down onto the lawn. "To heck with her. She stole all that jewelry, and I'm going to turn her in. I don't even like her. And what's it to you, fat face? Do *you* like her? You *do*. That's it! I call her Pedilia Pickle." Harvey laughed at that, as if he thought it was pretty clever. His laughter sounded screechy, like the shriek of a giant bat caught in a net. He stopped laughing suddenly, getting mad again. "And don't tell me what to do," he said. Then he picked up one of Danny's marbles and shot it very hard into the ring. All of a sudden playing marbles wasn't fun any more.

Harvey Chickel was too big. He was a year older than John and three years older than Danny. He liked that, because being the oldest and the biggest, he got to be the boss. He liked to be the boss, and would get mad if he couldn't be. He knew about fighting, or thought he did, and always liked to teach it to John and Danny.

What he *really* liked to do, though, was push them over and then stand there making grunting noises and waving his hands as they do in movies. He called it karate, but it was just being mean, and being stupidly mean, too. Both John and Danny knew that, but there didn't seem to be anything they could do about it.

And he liked to swordfight with sticks, using trashcan lids for shields. It was a fun enough idea, of course, except that what he wanted to do was bash Danny with his sword. Then he would say he hadn't meant to, and that Danny hadn't used his shield right and so it was *his* fault and was a good lesson. Somehow when Harvey came around there was always trouble, but it was never his fault.

23

Harvey didn't pick on John as much, because John was almost as big as he was and might put up too much of a fight if he was pushed too far. It was more fun for Harvey to pick on littler kids, who couldn't very well fight back. Harvey wrecked the marble game. He wanted to play 'for keeps' he said. He would borrow marbles from both of them and then give back the marbles he borrowed and keep the marbles he won. John was smart enough to see that there was something wrong with the idea. Harvey would go home with marbles when he hadn't brought any over. And John could tell that Danny simply didn't want Harvey to play at all. He wanted Harvey to go home, and to do it right now.

So Harvey got mad and said they were selfish. Then he said he wanted to wrestle. Because neither John nor Danny wanted to, he got even madder and kicked the marbles all over the place and erased the circle in the dirt. The dog Ahab chased the marbles around, still thinking they were bugs. Harvey laughed at that and said that Ahab was stupid, which he wasn't, of course. Then he started throwing the marbles out onto the lawn, screaming at Ahab to fetch them back. In a minute, half of the marbles were lost. Harvey said he was tired of playing. "I'm bored," he said, grinning at them.

John was about to explode, but he didn't want to, because that's what Harvey wanted him to do. John didn't want to fight with Harvey, or yell at him, or tell him to go home. That would just make things worse. John didn't like to fight with anyone. He wanted everything to be friendly and cheerful—always. Besides, Harvey was too big—big enough to be scary. And Harvey *liked* fighting and yelling. That's what he did best.

They were saved, though, because their mother called out the back door that it was dinner time and for them to come in and for Harvey to go home. After dinner there was enough light left for them to search out some of the lost marbles. When they put them into the fishbowl, though, it wasn't as full as it had been when they had started the marble game. They emptied their jewel box marbles back into it, and that helped a little bit, but not much. John could see that Danny was upset. They were really *his* marbles, after all. He had paid for them with his good luck penny. So John very quickly said that tomorrow morning they would look for marbles again, and get Ahab's help to do it. Ahab would 'sniff them out,' he said.

Then it occurred to John that it might be all right if they *didn't* find all the marbles, but instead found them by accident, one at a time, in the weeks and months to come. It would be like coming upon a treasure, wouldn't it? Danny thought about it for a minute and said that maybe it would, and he was happy enough at the idea of such a thing.

So they took out their jewel box marbles again, and put them back into the boxes. The fishbowl didn't seem *quite* as empty as it had seemed, because it was filled with the promise of the marbles that they might find tomorrow or the next day or some day next summer.

Danny put on the spectacles and grinned at John, making a face.

"They make your eyes green," said John.

"Like in Oz," Danny said, taking off the glasses. John pulled the curtain aside and peered out into the night. It was dark outside. The moon wasn't up yet. There was just the glow of the porchlamp shining across roses and begonias and wisteria vines. The light was pale green, as if they were under the ocean.

Danny gave John the spectacles and then sat down on the desk chair. "I don't like Harvey," he said.

John shrugged. He didn't like Harvey either, not really. When Harvey was around, though, it was easier to get into trouble. And getting into trouble was fun, sometimes, until you got yelled at for it or sent to your room. The real problem with Harvey, John thought, was that he went too far. If only he didn't go too far. There was a part of Harvey that liked adventures and eating and climbing trees. It was just that the bad parts of him made you forget about the good parts.

It would be good, John thought, if you could get rid of the bad parts—just erase them. There was a lot of stuff he would get rid of in himself, starting with the way he was afraid of Harvey. Then he would get rid of the way he was afraid of the dark, and . . . He decided to quit thinking of things that he was afraid of. "Oh Harvey's all right," he said. "You just have to understand him. He's just a show off."

"Well I don't like him," Danny said again. He couldn't put it any more clear than that. "He can't play with my marbles any more."

"That's right," John said. "We'll keep them away from him."

"He'll steal them next. I know he will."

"No he won't," said John, trying on the spectacles. He looked around the room, imagining that he was on the bottom of the sea and that the chair and toybox and bookcase and bunkbeds were caves in rock reefs and that the toys scattered on the floor were fish that lived in the caves. "We won't let him, like I said. Let's hide our jewel boxes on the top shelf, behind the books."

That seemed to be a good idea to Danny, and so both of them got busy on it and found hiding places in the bedroom that were secret enough so that Harvey wouldn't find the boxes, not even if he knew that there *were* boxes, which he didn't. Each of them kept out his good luck marble, though—the Christmas marble and the Easter marble—to carry in his pocket.

John put the spectacles on the window sill, and the fishbowl on the dresser. Then the two of them got ready for bed. After they had brushed their teeth, their father and mother came in and all of them read their favourite G. Smithers' book, which was about some of the adventures of the Man in the Moon. It started with a rhyme, like this:

'There was a man lived in the moon, lived in the moon, lived in the moon.
There was a man lived in the moon,
And his name was Aiken Drum.'

CHAPTER THREE

THROUGH THE BEDROOM WINDOW

The sun shined on Sunday morning. John and Danny woke up late. When he sat up in the top bunk, John was surprised to see a sort of green rainbow on the wall, like sunlight slanting through an aquarium. It was coming from the spectacles on the windowsill. Light bounced through them and washed across the floor and wall. He rubbed his eyes and watched.

Something seemed to be moving through the light—leafy trees, maybe, waving in a wind, or clouds sailing through a sky. Specks of dust floated through, like tiny autumn leaves. Then a cloud moved across the sun outside, and the green light dimmed and was gone. There had been some sort of magic in the light.

They got dressed in mess-around clothes, and after that they pushed some toys under the bed in order to straighten the room. Then, for no reason at all, John picked up the spectacles and put them on, pulling the curtain aside and looking out the window. There was the moon, high in the sky again. He shouted and jumped backward, but not because of the moon. Danny shouted too, because John had stepped on his toe. Then John pulled the spectacles off and rubbed his eyes. He stepped back away from the window, gave Danny an odd look, and put them back on.

What he saw was very curious. The wall of their bedroom was gone. The toybox, the desk, the window curtains were gone. There was only the green-tinted window—Mrs. Owlswick's window—sort of floating in the air. The bedroom had vanished around him. He could still catch a glimpse of it out of the corner of his eye if he looked sideways past the edge of the spectacles. But *through* the spectacles there was nothing but the window, floating there.

And beyond, as if the window were a framed picture, John saw an oakwoods with a stream running out of it. The porch was gone, along with the wisteria vines and rose bush. The front yard was a meadow strewn with wildflowers. A tall house with three chimneys sat distant and lonesome on a far-off hill. He had seen the house before, a picture of it, maybe. But he couldn't right then remember when. There were mountains farther off, beyond the house, bending around and falling away toward a big wash of blue-green, that might be the sky or might be the sea.

The world through the window was almost round, as if it sat on the inside of a very clear marble or on the inside wall of a fishbowl. In an instant John had flipped the catch on Mrs. Owlswick's window and pushed the window open.

"What are you doing?" asked Danny. "Let me try the glasses."

"I'm opening the window," John said. "There's something funny outside. Hold on."

"There's nothing funny outside, except Penny, the cat. Let me try them."

John shook his head. "Wait." After a moment he took the spectacles off, looking puzzled, and handed them to Danny. Then he sat down on Danny's bed while Danny looked out at the meadow and the house on the hill.

"What is it?" Danny asked. "What's happened? It's like a movie on the glasses or something."

"I don't think so," John said. "It's real."

"I'm going to find out," Danny said. "You can wait here if you want to."

Ahab wandered into the room just then and started nosing around the floor, as if he had come in looking for something, and had forgotten what it was. "We're not supposed to climb out the window," John said, but Danny

had already leaned across the sill and started to crawl out. He kept on going. "We can if there's a fire."

"There isn't any fire. We're going to get into trouble." It was too late, though. Danny was out the window. It looked to John, who didn't have the spectacles on, as if Danny had simply disappeared. Ahab put his paws on the windowsill and looked out, sniffing the air.

Danny's voice came through the window, "Take a look," he said. Then a strange thing happened. Danny's arm, all by itself, shoved in through the open window. It stayed there, sort of hanging for a second, floating in the air and holding onto the spectacles. Then, before John could grab them, the arm started to jerk them back. It was as if Danny wanted to keep them, and didn't want John to have a look through them. So John grabbed them away quick. It was *his* turn, after all. If there was something funny going on out there, he wanted to see it too, and if Danny kept the glasses to himself, he was more likely to get into trouble.

But when John grabbed them, Danny's hand disappeared altogether. Now there was no Danny at all. It was as if he had crawled under the house and was gone. John slipped the spectacles on and shoved his head out the window. There was his brother, down below, not sitting on begonias or pulling himself out of rosebushes, but lying on the high grass of the meadow, looking surprised. He blinked at John and sat up.

John looked around. He still couldn't quite believe what he saw. There were the oak woods, the stream, the house on the hill. He pulled his head back into the room and took the glasses off. The bedroom was as it had been—a little messy, as usual, but very much their bedroom.

Holding the spectacles in his hand, John looked outside again. There was nothing out there now but what ought to be outside: the porch, the potted plants, the hanging vines—everything but Danny. Danny wasn't there. So John started to put the glasses back on. It scared him to do it, but he had to know where his brother was.

Then, just to see what would happen, he grabbed Ahab's collar and pulled him up to the window. Ahab blinked out, watching Penny the cat asleep on the porch swing. John put the glasses on Ahab, who looked very funny in them, and then he pulled the chair across to the window, boosted Ahab up onto it, and shouted, "Jump!" Ahab leaped through happily, wearing the spectacles.

Now John was more frightened than ever. He didn't know where the spectacles had gone. Like Danny, Ahab had disappeared. Penny still slept on the swing, and John was all alone in the bedroom, having lost his brother and his dog.

He suddenly decided to get his mother and father. He would be in trouble for sure—messing around with magic spectacles, pushing Ahab out through the open window, losing his brother—but he would be in more trouble if he did nothing.

Just when he turned to go, though, there was Danny's head, in at the window again, wearing the glasses. Ahab had brought them to him. "C'mon," he said to John. "What are you waiting for?"

John shook his head. "Not me," he said. "I think we better give the glasses back to the man at the store. I don't think we ought to have them. He must not have known they were magical or something."

"Of course he knew," Daniel said. "He knows everything. You can tell it just to look at him."

Well, that much was probably true. But they were in trouble already, or *maybe* they were, anyway. There was no way that John was going to make it worse, not now. Just then Danny was pulled from behind, nearly out of the window.

"Wait!" he said, half turning around. Then to John he said, "It's Ahab. He wants to chase rabbits. I'm holding on to his collar."

"Are there rabbits out there?" asked John.

"Of course there's rabbits. And probably deer, too. And a forest, and mountains. You saw it, didn't you?"

John nodded and bit his lip, which is what he did when he wasn't sure about things. "Maybe . . ." he said.

"Maybe nothing, come on. Only for a second."

"I'm going to bring some stuff," he said.

"What stuff? We don't need any stuff. We aren't going

30

anywhere far. Leave it, will you?" Danny was starting to get mad. In a moment, if John didn't join him, he would go off by himself, with Ahab, and John would miss out on the adventure altogether. Danny looked like a head with glasses on, jerking backward and half disappearing when Ahab pulled on him. "Say," Danny said, giving in just a little. "Get some cookies. And some granola bars and raisins and bananas and bring *them* along. We'll need a lunch."

"Lunch!" said John. The idea of lunch was crazy. They hadn't even eaten breakfast yet.

Danny nodded. "Just get it. And don't tell mom and dad. We'll be back quick enough. We'll just have a look at the stream. If there's fish in it, we'll catch a mess of them and take them back with us and surprise them."

John liked the notion of catching fish from a stream. Suddenly the idea of exploring the magical land started to seem pretty good. "I'll get the big aquarium net," he said, "and the backpack and our jackets and . . ." Then Danny slipped backward, out the window, and was gone.

John rushed over and shoved his head out. Of course he couldn't see anything strange without the glasses on, just the front porch and all. He backed up and there was Danny again, looking in. Danny said, "I slipped off. I had to pile up some branches in order to get up high enough. The window is farther up from the ground outside than it is from the floor inside."

John nodded, in a hurry now to get out the window himself. It seemed to be an easy enough thing to climb back and forth between the bedroom and wherever it was that Danny and Ahab were. There was nothing to it. Nothing would go wrong. They'd be back quick, after taking a little look around. He bit his lip again as he dashed away toward the kitchen. Their mom was busy—upstairs, maybe. Their dad was in the garage, cutting up wood to build a bookcase. They'd think he and John were around the corner at Joseph's house or down the street at Colin's.

There were apple pies baking in the kitchen, and the smell of them was wonderful. John wished that he could take one along, but of course he couldn't, so he grabbed

31

four granola bars instead, and two bananas and two apples and six cookies. Then he grabbed six more cookies, just to be safe, and some cheese and raisins and, proud of himself for thinking of it, a handful of Halloween candy from each of their bags. He went back out into the livingroom and there was his mother, coming down the stairs.

"Have you seen my green Christmas pin?" she asked. "The one with all the red jewels, like holly berries? I can't find it anywhere."

"No," said John. "I haven't seen it. Maybe Danny has." He snatched up their jackets and backpacks and was back in the bedroom quick, handing the stuff to Danny who hauled it out the window.

Then Danny's hand appeared again, holding the spectacles, waving them around. John took them and put them on, checked to see that his good luck marble was in his pocket, and leaned out through the window, sliding out in a rush. Danny half-caught him and the two of them tumbled over backward onto the meadow. There was Ahab, chasing around through the tall grass.

The air was clean and fine and full of the brown, musty smell of oak trees and distant pruning fires and with the smell of the ocean. It was warm enough so that they tied their jackets around their waists, and would have taken off their shoes and tied them through their belt loops, except that they didn't want *too* much stuff tied around their waists, and also, the meadow was a little too rocky for bare feet.

Their bedroom window, Mrs. Owlswick's window, still hung in the air above the meadow. It just floated there—an open, wood-frame window, painted white, without any wall around it, without any house eaves slanting down over it. John, who still had the spectacles on, could see it, but Danny couldn't. Danny knew where the window *probably* was hanging, because he had piled up two or three broken-off tree branches beneath it, and the tree branches were still there.

"Can you see the window?" Danny asked.

"Yes," said John. "And I can see the bedroom through it, but not around it."

32

Danny nodded. "I know," he said. "*I* can't see the window at all, not without the spectacles on."

That was scary—the idea of not being able to see the window at all. John decided not to take the spectacles off. "Let's put more stuff here," he said. "More branches."

But just then Ahab started to bark like crazy, and he ran off down a little path that led toward the woods. A big, long-eared rabbit ran along in front of him, jumping off the path and into the grass, leaping into the bushes that grew along the edge of the meadow and into the shadow of the woods. Ahab followed it into the leafy darkness and was gone.

Danny jumped up and ran down the path after him, shouting Ahab's name. John ran behind him, holding the spectacles in his hand, no longer worrying about the window. He didn't want to be left alone, not right then. And it would be terrible if Ahab got lost, especially in a magical land. Ahab didn't know anything about windows or glasses or piles of wood. He needed John and Danny. And both of them knew that they needed him just as much. Ahab was big enough so that he made you feel safe, and he was smart, too. Or at least he was careful. He wouldn't go into the street or farther away from home than Shirley's house next door, where Penny the cat lived.

Except now he had lost his head and gone off chasing a rabbit, and so when he *would* try to find his way home, there wouldn't be any familiar street or neighbours' houses or anything like that. Without the glasses, he wouldn't even see the window in the air.

In a moment John and Danny were in the woods, walking along down a path of weedy sand. It was quiet and cool in the shade of the trees. Here and there was a patch of what appeared to be old pavement, as if maybe a street had run through the woods ages ago and was slowly being crumbled and buried by the forest. The oak trees around them were old and big, with long, tangled limbs, so that only a little bit of sunlight shined through to the forest floor.

They could hear Ahab crashing around ahead. He barked once, then growled, then fell suddenly silent so that John and Danny hurried along to see what the matter was. Some way into the woods, when the meadow had disappeared behind them and there was nothing but shadows and the creaking of branches and the dark forest silence, they found themselves in a clearing that was almost round. There was a stone ring in the middle of it, cracked and old and covered with vines.

It might have been a fountain once, very much like the one in the Plaza at home, but that would have been an awfully long time ago, to be sure. A trickle of dirty water gurgled out of it, flowing off into the muddy sand. Everything was silent for a moment, and then there was the crashing of something off in the brush again. They couldn't see what it was. Of course it must have been Ahab. It wasn't a bear or a lion or anything.

John stood very close to Danny, and both of them listened and looked hard into the trees. "Ahab?" said John. Then, louder, he shouted, "Ahab!" and Ahab came leaping out of the bushes, glad as could be to see them, and bounced straight into them wagging his tail.

Danny stumbled backward into John, and John fell straight over onto the path, sitting down hard. The spectacles flew out of his hand, spinning through the air and smashing up against the ring of stone. John jumped to his feet and snatched them up from where they had fallen on the sandy ground and held them by the wire frame.

One of the green lenses was gone. There was nothing but an empty circle of wire where there used to be a lens. It must have flown out into the grass or something. Maybe it had broken, but they couldn't see any pieces of it at all.

Both of them started to search through the grass, but before John had got very far he thought of something that made him stop. It didn't make things better, though; it made things worse. He looked at the spectacles, then looked at Danny and said, "What if Mom shuts the window and latches it?"

Danny didn't say anything. John stood up and took hold of Ahab's collar, starting back up the path toward the meadow. Suddenly the idea of messing around in the magical land didn't seem half as good an idea to him as it had. Both of them started to run.

34

CHAPTER FOUR

WHAT HAPPENED ON THE MEADOW

The window wasn't there any more.

The quiet breeze stirred the meadow grasses, and a leaf drifted past. The air was suddenly lonesome and strange. Even Ahab stood still and glanced around uneasily. Something seemed to have changed.

There was the heap of branches on the ground, sitting just where Danny had piled them up. John put on the spectacles and looked around. Maybe the window had moved, he thought. Maybe the wind had blown it, like a kite, and it was someplace else now—off toward the woods or farther along across the meadow or down toward the sea. He put his hand over the half of the spectacles that had no lens, so that the land and sky were watery green. But everything he saw seemed flat, like a painting on a screen. The magic seemed to have gone out of the spectacles, and the window was gone.

"Let me try them," Danny said. He sounded worried. More leaves drifted past. The sun was sliding down the back of the sky toward afternoon, and the full moon was high and bright. "I can't see anything either." He climbed up onto the pile of branches, holding on with one hand and feeling around in the air with the other. But there was nothing. They both knew, somehow, that there would be nothing. Broken spectacles wouldn't work.

They were in a mess, for sure, but it didn't seem to John that he had done anything to deserve being in a mess. They had crawled out the window, of course, but that wasn't a really *bad* thing to do. And they had gone off without telling their mother or father where it was they were going, but that wasn't really as bad as it was dumb. And they hadn't wanted to be gone long or to go very far. They had been able to see the stream from their bedroom window, after all. It was like going across the street. But as soon as he thought about his bedroom window and about his mother and father and about his street, it all seemed about twice as terrible.

A sycamore leaf blew past on the wind just then, nearly bumping John's nose. More leaves followed—a dozen of them, like boats in the air. They were shaped something like dried stars with the points turned up and painted autumn colours. Ahab started to bark. John, who was sitting on a branch wondering what to do next, said, "What?" because he thought at first that Ahab could see the window again.

What Ahab had seen, though, were little men riding on the leaves—men as small as your thumb.

They wore tiny vests and broad-brimmed black hats, and most of them were plump and looked as if they loved to eat. They weren't smiling much, though, and were holding onto the stems of the leaves as if the stems were tillers and they were steering their leaf-boats along a river of air.

In the middle of the leaves, in a heap between their crossed legs, were little piles of coloured glass chips, shining in the afternoon sunshine.

They were henny-penny men, is what they were, right out of a G. Smithers book. They stared at John, who sat there looking astonished and still wearing the broken spectacles. In a second they were swirling around and around his head, like a little wind devil of leaves. Then away they flew on the wind, rising and falling and whirling in a great curvy path across the meadow until they disappeared in the distance, off in the direction of the cottage on the far-off hill.

When the henny-pennies had gone, the air was doubly quiet—a late afternoon sort of quiet. The wind that blew felt suddenly like an evening wind.

John shivered, and Ahab rubbed against his leg, looking around himself at the grass sighing in the wind, as if he thought that the meadow was a lonesome place too.

"Why did they have all the broken glass?" Danny asked.

John shrugged. "I don't know."

"What if part of it was pieces of our spectacles?"

"Why would they have taken the pieces of our spectacles?" John asked.

"Why are they carrying broken glass at all?" asked Danny.

John didn't say anything. He was thinking. He knew all at once that the worst thing they could do was stand there on the meadow worrying and thinking. What if night came, and they had no place to sleep? They had enough food to eat for the moment, but after that, what then? What about breakfast? they had to be moving. They had to try to do something, or else things would just get worse and worse.

Thinking about tomorrow's breakfast had made things worse already, because that meant thinking about spending the night in the open in a strange land, and that meant not finding their way home again, and that meant . . . He made himself stop wondering what that meant. They had to *do* something, not sit and think.

"Where did the henny-penny men go, do you think?" asked Danny, holding onto Ahab's collar and trying to be brave.

"To that house, I guess." John pointed at the cottage on the hill. It wasn't a bad looking cottage. That is to say, it didn't look haunted or anything. It was rather nice, in fact, with three chimneys and with windows that reflected sunlight, and green lawns falling away down the hill, and flowers growing up in broad flowerbeds. A weather vane on top pointed up the valley, toward the distant mountains. It didn't seem very likely that bad people could live in a good house. If they did, then the house would turn bad too; but this house obviously hadn't. That's what John was thinking, anyway.

"Let's go there, too," Danny said. "The henny-pennies are good people, aren't they?"

"In G. Smithers' books they are, I guess. I don't know what they do, really."

"Where else can we go?"

John thought. Then he said, "We've got to go back and find the lens of the broken spectacles. They couldn't have got all the pieces so fast. That's what we've got to do, before it's lost. Maybe we can put the spectacles back together. The window's still there, I'm certain of it. Maybe all we need is a *piece* of the green glass."

Ahab, as if he understood, trotted away toward the woods again, and Danny turned around and followed. Both boys looked back at the heap of brush on the meadow a couple of times. John was hoping that they would see the window again, hoping that they weren't trapped in the magic land like it seemed they were. But no window appeared; there was just the quiet, empty meadow.

The woods were darker and spookier. The sun was low in the sky, so that the trees cast long shadows, and the breeze blew the branches high up in the trees and made them dance and rustle. There were noises, too: the whoo-whooing of an owl and the chatter of squirrels.

Something stirred in the bushes, rustling around. "Probably just birds," John said to Danny, but something in him didn't really believe it. He listened hard, barely breathing, ready to turn around and run for the meadow.

"This is it, I think," said John, looking around them at the sandy trail and at the stone circle. "This is where they broke, right against the edge here." Around the circle, though, was nothing but sand and weeds. There was still no lens.

They got down onto their hands and knees and poked into the sand with their fingers. They crawled through the grass searching. But they couldn't find anything, not a single chip of green glass. The air seemed to be getting misty and wet, and the sun disappeared above them, behind a blanket of fog. John untied his jacket and put it on, then put the spectacles carefully into his jacket pocket. When he did, he saw a face peering out at them from behind a tree.

For a second John couldn't say anything at all. Then he

touched Danny's shoulder, very lightly, still watching the face. Danny said, "What?" and went on searching in the weeds and leaves. Then the face was gone.

At first John thought it had been the face of the little green-hatted man from the curiosity shop. But it hadn't been. It was too ugly—all wrinkly and green like an old dollar bill that has gone through the wash. It wasn't at all pleasant. There was more rustling in the brush.

"A face," John whispered.

Ahab tilted his head suspiciously, as if he, too, were starting to suspect that it wasn't just birds in the bushes.

Danny looked up at John and said, "What?" again, then very slowly turned to look where John was looking. There was no face there anymore. "I don't see a face," Danny whispered. But John knew that he couldn't have been imagining it. It had been real.

And besides, who had taken the missing lens? It was beginning to seem as if someone had, and very recently, too.

Ahab growled just then, and his fur stood up in a little line down his back. There was the unpleasant smell of dead fish in the air suddenly and what sounded like someone giggling.

"C'mon," whispered John, and they edged away down the trail, back out toward the meadow and the sunlight. They both held onto Ahab's collar with one hand and onto their backpacks with the other. It wouldn't do to have Ahab go bolting off into the woods again.

They hadn't taken three steps, though, when out stepped a tiny man, not much taller than John's belt buckle. He stood in the middle of the path grinning. He was bald on top, and the hair around his ears was thin and wispy and it stood away from his head as if it were electrified. When he opened his mouth and smiled wider, his teeth were pointed, like the teeth of an animal.

He wore odd clothes, too—clothes that seemed to be stitched up out of the skins of birds, or maybe bats, and his shoes didn't quite match. In fact, his shoes weren't shoes at all; they were the empty skins of rats, with the long tails tied up around his ankles like the straps of sandals.

He clearly wasn't simply a little man; not really. He was a goblin. He held out his hand to them.

After a moment of looking at the open hand, Danny whispered, "What does he want?"

"Money, maybe," said John.

Ahab growled, very low in his throat, as if he didn't like goblins who wore rats for shoes.

John reached into his pocket and found eight cents—three pennies and a nickel. It wasn't much, but maybe if the goblin knew that it was all they had, he would let them pass. And besides, what did goblins know about money? John reached the coins out to him, taking a step forward but not wanting to get *too* close. Immediately the goblin smacked the coins out of John's hand, into the brush along the trail, and then laughed hard, sounding like a turkey.

"Hey!" shouted John, getting mad. Ahab pulled forward, yanking both Danny and John along with him, and the goblin leaped away into the trees and was gone.

"Quick!" John shouted, starting out again, and Danny ran alongside. They were almost to the meadow when the goblin appeared again, this time with three more goblins, all just like him. They jumped out in front of the boys, right smack in the middle of the trail. One had a fishbone stuck in his hair like a comb, and another wore a piece of fishing line tied around his neck, with three old glass prisms hanging from it. The other had a jewelled pin stuck like a badge to his raggedy shirt. It was a green Christmas wreath, with red rhinestones in the green, like holly berries.

"Hey!" John shouted. "That's mom's pin! That's the one she lost!"

The goblin that had swatted away the money shoved out his hand again, just for a moment. Then he made circles of his thumbs and fingers and held them over his eyes. Then he held out his hand again. The other goblins nodded their heads and made turkey noises, and one of them—the one with the prisms—made circles of his fingers and thumbs too, but poked himself in the eye by mistake and shouted.

One of the other three laughed, and the one with the poked eye reached across and yanked the Christmas pin off the other's shirt and tried to shove it into his own pocket.

The third goblin snatched it away, though, and poked the prism goblin in the ear with his finger, and suddenly the three of them were yowling and hissing and poking and scratching and pulling at prisms and pins and hitting each other on the nose. The first goblin, the one holding out his hand, didn't seem a bit surprised, but just stood there, giving John and Danny a hard look.

Suddenly John knew what the goblin wanted. He started to reach for the spectacles, which were zipped into his jacket pocket. He didn't reach for them in order to give them to the goblin, but to make sure they were safe. He stopped, though, and dropped his hands to his side. If he went reaching for the spectacles, then the goblin would know that he had them and might try to take them away.

Ahab barked—straight into the goblin's face. The three that were wrestling around gave off and looked up, surprised. Ahab barked again, and the goblin took a step back, nearly kicking his companions, who were tangled up on the ground. Then Ahab charged at them, growling and barking, as if he'd had enough of them and was clearing them out.

The goblins jumped up and ran for it, down the path for about ten steps, howling and gobbling and waving their arms before crashing off into the bushes and disappearing. John and Danny held onto Ahab's collar the whole way. They dragged along behind him and yelled at him to slow up, which he didn't do until they were back out on the meadow. Almost at once they saw goblin faces at the edge of the woods again. And there weren't just three or four of them now, but a dozen, peeking here and there past trees and out of bushes.

Ahab started to growl again, and made a dash at them, but John called him back, and he came. The goblins were gone for an instant. Then they crept back, first one, then another, then a whole batch of them. All of them were dressed in the same sorts of raggedy, outlandish bat shirts and rat shoes and rhinestone jewelry, and with their hair wild and windblown. They wouldn't come out of the shadow of the woods and fog, into the sunshine of the meadow.

41

"What do they want?" asked Danny. "Are goblins good, like the henny-pennies?"

John shook his head. He hadn't *heard* of goblins being good anyway. Generally, in G. Smithers books, they were up to mischief, kicking over cans of paint or stealing berries or leaving smelly old half-eaten fish in someone's well. "They want the spectacles. Didn't you see that one make glasses out of his fingers and thumbs?"

There was still no window on the meadow, and the sun was almost gone, swallowed up by the distant hills. "Let's go," Danny said to John. "Up to that house on the hill. Before it gets dark." Then he stood up and set out, and John had no choice but to follow, although that's pretty much what he wanted to do anyway. He had discovered long ago that when Danny wanted to do something he usually did it, alone if he had to. Truthfully, though, Danny always seemed happier to have John's company. And right now, John wanted Danny's company too. So they hurried across the grass with Ahab trotting in front and every once in a while barking at the woods. The meadow was almost dark when they reached the foot of the hill.

The coming of night made them move along faster yet. John began thinking that it wasn't very much fun being out alone with darkness falling and them not knowing where they were. At home, on Pine Street, the streetlights would be coming on just about then, when it had gotten too dark to play outside any more and when it was only ten or fifteen minutes away from night-time. John forced himself to quit thinking again. He didn't need any more worries than he already had.

The road they travelled didn't have any streetlights, though, just thick trees along either side—trees that might easily be full of goblins. They could see lights on in the cottage now, upstairs and downstairs both, and there was the smell of food cooking and the sound of someone laughing and then someone else talking very loud, although John and Danny were too far away to hear what was said. The smell of food reminded John of what they had in their backpacks, which they had forgotten all about in their troubles.

"What did you bring?" asked Danny. "Anything good? Not those old bananas, I hope, with the brown spots all over them." It was pretty clear that John had, though, because the backpack smelled like bananas.

John said he liked bananas that way, although he didn't want one now. What he did want was a granola bar and then some Halloween candy. John wondered why they were whispering to each other. They were in among the roadside trees, and so couldn't see the house above them any longer. They could still hear the talk though, along with a lot of laughter, which made the night a little more cheerful than it might have been.

The candy rolled around in the bottom of the backpack, and John gathered it up with his hand. He was just getting set to ask Danny what it was that he wanted, Smarties or a Hershey bar or Sugar Babies, when from out of the trees on their right came a frightful gobbling and yowling. There was a smashing and crackling of brush and the patter of dozens of little rat-clad feet, and suddenly the road ahead of them was full of goblins, a dozen of them, all capering and dancing and shrieking and tearing down at the boys in a rush.

CHAPTER FIVE

THE FIGHT ON THE ROAD

Ahab leaped straight into the mob of goblins, nearly pulling Danny over onto his face and knocking the little men this way and that way across the road. But there were too many of them for one dog to scare off, and they came yowling around, almost all of them making the glasses sign with their fingers. John threw his handful of candy straight at them and shouted, then turned to run back down the hill, toward the distant meadow.

When John looked back, he could see Danny standing in the middle of a mob of goblins, slamming at them with the backpack, the granola bars and bananas sailing out onto the road. One of the backpack straps caught around a goblin's neck, and when the little man jerked away he pulled it out of Danny's hand and tried straightaway to see what was in it, but couldn't because it was still caught around his neck. Four or five of the other goblins began pulling on it trying to help.

"Run!" John shouted.

And if Danny had turned around right then and run for it, he would have got clear away, just as John had, but instead he shouted, "Hey!" and went after his backpack. In a second the goblins had grabbed onto his legs and arms like smelly monkeys, and little goblin hands were snaking into his jacket pockets. Danny fought hard to pull away and throw them off, but his fighting was useless, and John could see that it was from where he stood down the hill,

45

wanting to run farther, down onto the meadow, and wanting just as badly to run back up the hill to help his brother. He felt as if he were frozen there.

When he heard Danny shouting, he knew he had to help him. If he ran farther away, it would be the worst thing that he had ever done in his life. He hollered at the goblins to leave Danny alone, and then he hollered, "Give it to them!" but it was clear that with all the goblins dancing around him, Danny couldn't 'give it' to anyone at all. John's legs felt as if they were made of dough, and his heart pounded, but he forced himself up the hill toward his brother. Shouting wouldn't do any good. The only right thing was to charge in. "Hey!" he yelled, and started to run.

There was another shout—but not from John or Danny or Ahab—from someone coming along fast down the road. There was a bang! and a kind of a whoosh, like a firecracker going off in a bathtub. Then the most amazing-looking man appeared, wearing a hat and carrying a gun. He threw the gun to his shoulder and shot up into the trees, and a great lot of what looked like fog flew out of the gun, smelling like soap in the breeze that blew the fog down toward them.

John reached Danny and the goblins first, slamming two of them down just by running over them. He reached into the crowd that held onto Danny's jacket, and grabbed hold of two more by the collars of their bat shirts. They clung to Danny like apes, though, and the two John had run over latched onto John's legs and fumbled in his pockets, trying to rob him.

"Help!" John yelled, kicking and twisting. He could see lamplight bouncing through the trees up toward the house, and right then the man with the gun arrived, puffing and out of breath. He was too fat, maybe, to do a lot of running, but he could yell easily enough, and the first thing he yelled was, "I'll shoot! Back away!"

The goblins weren't listening. They had given up trying to carry either of the boys away, but wanted only to rob them of something. John knew what it was, and he fought to keep them away from his jacket pocket, hoping that the

man knew what he was doing with the gun and wouldn't start shooting things up.

He didn't start to shoot, though. He poked at goblins with the gun barrel, jabbing it this way and that way and making them leap and shout, and he grabbed onto the loose bits of their bat shirts and pulled on them, hauling goblins away and dropping them onto the road.

Danny jerked his arm loose now, and he started to pull the little men off, with Ahab and John helping out. John dragged the goblins away two at a time toward the forest, wrinkling his nose at their awful fishy smell and all the time not letting any of the little men around behind him where they might dig for the glasses in his pocket. His heart was still thumping, but his legs didn't feel like dough anymore because he hadn't any time to think about how his legs felt.

The truth was, though, that he didn't feel very brave at all, or even happy that they were chasing off the goblins. He felt ashamed of himself. But he wasn't ashamed of himself for running off when he should have stayed. He really had thought that Danny would follow him. What he didn't like is that he had waited on the road when he should have run back to help his brother. Why had he stood there and done all that stupid yelling? It should have been *him*, and not the mysterious man from up the road, who had been able to rescue Danny, but all the bravery and fighting in the world wouldn't make up for that now.

And then all of a sudden the goblins were gone, back toward the woods, and John and Danny and Ahab were safe on the road. Ahab barked one last time at the goblins' backs. It wasn't clear what had finally scared them off.

Danny gathered up the backpack from where it had fallen on the road. "Look!" he shouted, pointing behind them all.

There, in the dust of the roadway, two goblins sat shoving Halloween candy into their mouths, not bothering to unwrap the pieces first. They smelled as if they had been wrestling with dead fish and hadn't taken a bath afterward, and their hair was something more like spider web than hair. There were sticky candy smears all over their faces, and one of them, screwing up his eyes, shoved a long, bony finger into his mouth and pulled out a drooly piece of plastic candy wrapper. He looked at it for a moment and then ate it. The night was silent now, except for their slobbering.

"Here now!" said the man with the gun, walking up to them and giving them a look. He poked one of them with his finger and jerked his head toward the woods. The two goblins looked around them as if they were very surprised to find their friends gone, but they still sat there, picking at the candy. They would have been merely silly, if they weren't so awfully smelly and dirty and if they weren't wearing dead rats for shoes. "Get along with you –" the man started to say.

But then there was a shout from behind them. John whirled around at the sound of the words, "Look out!" and there was a woman with a lantern, ten yards away, up the hill, pointing her finger toward the edge of the woods. The two candy-eaters leaped up from the road, cackling like turkeys as the rest of the goblins raged out of the trees in a wild charge, whooping and gobbling and tripping over each other.

"Behind me!" yelled the man with the gun, who took a step forward, aimed his weapon at the wild goblins, and pulled the trigger.

There was a sound like sand being poured through a pipe, and a bump, bump, bump, bang, whoosh! that pitched the man over backward. He knocked into Danny, who sat down hard on the road.

The air was filled with smoke. Only it wasn't smoke; it was fog, wet and cold and smelling like soap. A wild shriek went up from the goblins, who smashed into each other trying to stop, all of them jumping around and knocking each other down. Then, in one big crowd they ran off down the road into the darkness, making little slobbering noises.

The man with the gun yelled, "And don't come back!" He turned and squinted at Danny and John, nodding at them as if to call attention to the way he had dealt with the goblins. Lantern light glowed across their shoes right then, and the fog lifted and evaporated in the air, like steam.

They looked up at the woman with the lantern. She was grey-haired, very tall and neat and elegant. She reminded John of Kimberly's Aunt, Mrs. Owlswick. In fact, she looked so much like her that she might easily have been her sister.

The man with the soap gun took his hat off and bowed, although he was too fat to make much of a job of it. He was almost bald, too, under his hat, which was ringed with a band of oak leaves. His little bit of hair stuck up into the air as if a heavy wind were blowing out of his coat collar. He wore a vest and a pair of walking shorts and high socks folded down at the tops with ribbons at the folds. His coat looked very comfortable, but was a little thin at the elbows, having been worn pretty hard. The strange thing about him, though, is that he looked like an overgrown goblin, only very pleasant and well groomed, all except for his wild hair.

"I'm *Mister* Deener," he said, putting peculiar emphasis on the Mister part. "At your service."

"I'm John and this is Danny and this is Ahab," John said. Then he said, "At yours," just to be gentlemanly, and he bowed too.

"And this," said the man while gesturing toward the woman with the lantern, "is Mrs. Florence Popple, Polly's Aunty Flo, which is what everyone calls her. You might as well call her that too." He said this last sentence in such a way that it sounded as if they ought to call her that right now. John nodded at her to be agreeable, and Danny said, "Hi." She *was* something like Polly's aunt, especially because she looked to be just the sort of person who everyone would call Aunt Somebody. She might have been everyone's aunt.

"Your soap gun worked exceedingly well, Mister Deener," said Aunty Flo, shaking his hand. Then to the boys she said, "Mr. Deener is an inventor, a very great inventor. He fell upon the notion that a goblin would fear soap more than bullets, and he built this weapon, which he's just now gotten a chance to use for the first time. *Very* successful, I'd say."

Mr. Deener smiled at John and Danny as if all of them had agreed about the wonderful soap weapon. Then he said, "And you would be the Kraken brothers, then?"

49

"No," said Danny, speaking up. "Who did you say?"

"The Kraken brothers, the wife's nephews, come to help. I've been expecting them."

"Than you'll just have to go on expecting them, Mr. Deener," said Aunty Flo, "because this isn't them."

Mr. Deener tilted his head. "I must say it looks very much like them."

"We're John and Danny and Ahab, actually," said John. "I'm sorry."

The woman said that they hadn't any business being sorry, and then leaned over and whispered to them that Mr. Deener had been waiting for the Kraken brothers to arrive for something like ten years, and that just between the three of them, she didn't believe that there *were* any Kraken brothers, not really. They were Mr. Deener's imaginary friends. Then she touched the side of her head with her finger and winked.

Mr. Deener looked confused for a moment, as if he wondered why he had thought that John and Danny were the Kraken brothers. "I . . . I'm sorry," Mr. Deener said. "I thought . . . For a moment I thought . . ." But he didn't finish his thinking. He stood there looking sad, remembering something that he couldn't put into words.

"You don't have any business being sorry either, Mr. Deener," Aunty Flo said. "You're too often sorry, and it doesn't improve your spirits at all." She started out up the road right then, and the boys and Ahab followed along behind without having to be asked first. There was nothing else to do on that dark night.

Mr. Deener tramped along behind, and in a moment he had forgotten his sorrow. It was gone, just like that, and Mr. Deener began humming and singing to himself and laughing at the song when he came to the good parts. Pretty soon there weren't any words left to the song at all, and he just laughed, ha, ha, ha, along with the melody. Two or three times he stopped, and said, "Hark!" and pointed the soap weapon at the woods. But there was no sign of any goblins, and in minutes they trudged around and onto a cobblestone carriage drive at the top of the hill. "Which of the brothers are you again?" Mr. Deener asked Danny, very abruptly, as if to catch him off guard, and squinting at him sideways.

"I'm Danny," Danny started to say, but he was interrupted by Aunty Flo, who said,

"These are *not* the brothers, Mr. Deener."

"Are they due tonight, then?"

"No," said Aunty Flo, "they are not." Then she stopped for a moment to think about something, and said finally. "Maybe these are the brothers after all." She turned to Danny and John and said, "Do you mind being Mr. Deener's imaginary friends?"

"No," John said. "I guess not. How imaginary do we have to be?"

Mr. Deener looked awfully happy for a moment, and he said, "Now that you've come, you don't have to be imaginary at all." They walked on a few paces, and he turned, looking puzzled again, and said, "Why *have* you come? That's what I'm wondering. I can't quite recall it."

"We don't know either," Danny said. "We just came."

"But the wife . . ." Mr. Deener started to say, but then stopped, as if the mention of 'the wife' had wrecked his thought. His face got the remembering look on it again. After a few moments, he smashed his eyes shut, pushing his cheeks up toward his forehead, so that all the feelings that were in his eyes and on his face got squashed out of it. When he opened his eyes he looked entirely pleasant and happy again.

Danny leaned over toward John and whispered, "Which wife?" But Aunty Flo shook her head at them, as if maybe they shouldn't say it very loud.

Mr. Deener turned happily to Aunty Flo and said, "I believe that this *is* them. I'm a stinker if I don't." Then he looked at them all and said, "Which of you calls me a stinker?"

"None of us calls you a stinker, Mr. Deener," Aunty Flo said. "On the contrary, you're rather a hero, aren't you, chasing the goblins off like that. Very brave, I call it."

"Well," he said, "maybe I am. But I didn't ask to be."

They walked across the cobbles of the drive, which were lit by oil lamps. Flowers bloomed in flowerbeds all around

51

the house, and the limbs of oak trees cast a tangle of shadows onto the ground. There was a big, well-lit front porch with trailing vines along it and with diamond-paned windows made of old, watery glass, very much like Mrs. Owlswick's window. Through one of them they could see a cheerful fire burning in a stone fireplace and a table set for dinner. A girl sat in a chair in front of the fire, sewing doll clothes. She put her needle and thread down when she heard them clump across the front porch and open the door.

CHAPTER SIX

GLAZED DOUGHNUTS

Ahab pushed past all of them and headed for the fire, wagging his tail at the girl as he went past. He curled up in front of the hearth and went straight to sleep.

"What a wonderful dog," she said, bending over to pat Ahab on the head. "What's his name?"

"Ahab," Danny said proudly. He had always liked the sound of that name.

"It sounds like the name of a king," she said.

But before Danny could explain that actually it was the name of a dog in a G. Smithers book, Aunty Flo said, "This is Polly." And Polly curtsied in an old fashioned way. John and Danny didn't know what to do about that, whether to bow or nod or just stand there feeling silly. Strangely enough, she looked a good deal like Kimberly, except her hair was shorter. And there was something else about her . . . Maybe it was that she was dressed a little bit old-fashioned too, in a blue dress with lace. Because she was pretty, it was about three times as hard to figure out something to say.

They didn't have to, though, because just then Mr. Deener took over and said to Polly, "These are the brothers, come to help. Their names, if I have it right, are John and Danny. And they're good, solid names, too. Not like some. We've routed a pack of goblins down on the road."

"The soap gun was a great success," said Aunty Flo.

Polly said, "I knew it would be," and she kissed Mr. Deener on the cheek, which made him sit down in the chair that Polly had been sitting in.

Just then someone who looked an awful lot like a ghost walked into the room from what must have been the direction of the kitchen. She was round and short, like a barrel, and pasty white, and she carried an enormous spoon.

"I've spilt the flour," she said, looking a little mad.

"Bother the flour," said Aunty Flo. "Scoop up what you can and sweep the rest into a box. We can make cakes for the squirrels with any that's got dirty."

She wasn't a ghost; she was just covered with flour. Mr. Deener looked very worried all of a sudden. "Cakes for the *squirrels?*" he said. "What about my cakes? Do I get a cake?"

"You'll get a dusty old clod," said the ghostly woman, evidently mad at having spilled the flour. But just then the smell of something baking—a pie, maybe, or a tray of cookies—came sailing out into the room, as if someone had opened an oven door.

Mr. Deener put his hand on his forehead and stood up. Then he moaned and sat back down, sinking low into his chair, so that his chin was pushed down into his chest and his eyes were squished into his cheeks again. "A dusty old clod," he said.

"Best not to start him up, Mrs. Barlow," said Aunty Flo to the flour woman.

Polly put a hand on Mr. Deener's shoulder. "You won't have to eat clods," she said to him. "I'll find you something nice. We'll find him something nice, won't we?"

John said, "Of course we will," and Danny said, "Sure."

Mr. Deener said, "A cake?"

"Of *course* there'll be cake," said Aunty Flo.

"And pies, I don't doubt?" Mr. Deener sat up straighter, cheering up at the idea of pies and cakes.

"He's starting up!" cried Aunty Flo. "Catch him!"

Mrs. Barlow rolled her eyes, then turned around and tramped away toward the kitchen.

Mr. Deener's fingers drummed on the arms of his chair. "And cookies," he said. He was clearly getting excited over

54

all the food talk. "And bread and cupcakes and honeycakes and curli-que rolls," he said. "And cinnamon twists and puffo-sweets and doughy delights and chocolate pinwheels!"

He got up and began to walk around the room, his eyes straight ahead of him, as if he was *thinking* about each treat one at a time and eating each one in his mind. But eating imaginary food seemed only to make him hungrier, and it made John and Danny hungrier too.

"Meringues," cried Mr. Deener. "Jelly rolls, cinnamon rolls, sugar rolls, milk-doggies, monkey bread, popovers, pollyannas, pinky winkys, polliwogs, popinjays, poppo-lumps . . ."

"Stop him, quick!" shouted Aunty Flo.

Polly clutched Mr. Deener's arm and tried to steer him back to his chair. But it was no use. He was wild with the idea of food, and he wouldn't sit down or keep still. He tried to rush toward the kitchen, but Polly still had hold of his arm, and Aunty Flo snatched up a handful of his coat. Mrs. Barlow came back out just then. "When the Deener is in one of his fits," she said to the boys, "it's no one but me who can settle him down. It's doughnuts that does it—glazeys only. No cake doughnuts."

She carried a long wooden dowel that was strung with glazed doughnuts, six or eight of them.

"I'll just have one of those," said Mr. Deener. "Two of them, maybe." He relaxed then, and Polly and Aunty Flo dragged him along back to his chair. "The pup will need one too," he said, whistling for Ahab, who looked up from his spot by the fire as if he were very happy to see the doughnuts. "And the brothers, of course." But he took the whole line of doughnuts away from Mrs. Barlow and began to eat them in two bites each, gulping them down and sort of wheezing, as if he were catching his breath. In a moment there wasn't a doughnut left, for Ahab or for anyone else.

"Well!" said Mrs. Barlow. "Aren't we a pig!"

Mr. Deener breathed heavily. His hands twitched on the arms of his chair. "I *am* ashamed," he said. "I was . . ."

"Overcome," said Polly helpfully. Then to John and Danny she said, "He can't help himself when the fit comes upon him. He must have doughnuts."

55

John nodded. He had felt that way himself a couple of times. "You have to keep a bunch of them around, then?"

"Oh, yes," said Polly. "Mrs. Barlow sees to that. She pretends that it makes her mad, but actually she makes the most lovely doughnuts." Then she whispered so that only they could hear her. "She's told me that she's trying to sweeten him up. She loves him, I think, but he makes her mad." She winked at them, and they nodded.

Danny whispered, "Won't he eat anything else?"

"Not when the fit's on him," Polly said. "When he has the fit, it's got to be glazed doughnuts. Aunty says it comes from remembering. Mr. Deener is what she calls a sufferer."

"Have we got any more?" Mr. Deener asked the cook. "Not for me, of course. I don't want them. I've eaten quite enough. You couldn't *make* me eat another one. Not if you tried." And with that he stopped talking and looked around, as if he were hopeful that someone would try to make him eat another doughnut. "I mean for the pup," he said. "And the brothers. Look at them, skinny as sticks. The goblins have the candy that they were bringing for me. It's a filthy shame. We must have another rod of glazeys."

"We know what your little game is, Deener," said Mrs. Barlow, giving him a look. "You'll snatch them up and eat them too, and the rest of us can go starve."

Ahab trotted over from his place by the fire and licked Mr. Deener's hand, which was all sugary from the doughnuts. Mr. Deener sighed deeply and said that Ahab understood him. And then Polly said that she understood him too. And Danny and John said that they did too, although actually John didn't understand much of anything except that he was awfully hungry all of a sudden. Mrs. Barlow left again, back into the kitchen, and came back out with another stick of doughnuts, which Mr. Deener tried to snatch out of her hands.

"Clods!" she shouted at him. "Dirt clods and muddy water!"

Mr. Deener collapsed into his chair, squishing up his cheeks and eyes again.

Mrs. Barlow passed out the doughnuts, two for each of them.

"Save two for . . . for the old man," said Mr. Deener suddenly, rising from his chair.

"He won't eat them," said Mrs. Barlow. "You know very well he won't. They'll sit by his bedside and dry out. I say we wake the old man up and *make* him eat one."

Aunty Flo said, "Never mind that. Right now the old man needs his sleep. The squirrels will eat the doughnuts right enough if he lets them dry out. Nothing will be wasted. Mr. Deener is quite right."

"I'll take them to him," said Polly, and she slipped the two glazed doughnuts off the dowel and hurried away toward a wooden stairs that angled up toward a second floor and then away toward a third. Mr. Deener looked very sad again.

"We'll eat supper backward tonight," said Aunty Flo. "We do that on Sundays. Dessert first."

"But we'll have dessert again after, of course," Mr. Deener whispered to John, and then shook his hand. The idea of dinner seemed to brighten him up. "Which of the brothers are you?"

"John."

"Pleased to meet you," said Mr. Deener. "I've been waiting for your arrival, you know. You have such an odd last name—Kraken. Do you know what a Kraken is?"

"No, sir," said John, who could see by now that it wasn't any use trying to tell Mr. Deener about his *real* last name, which certainly wasn't Kraken.

"It's a great sea creature—a squid or an octopus or something that pretends to be an island, and people come along on boats and pitch tents on it and eat picnic lunches, and then, in the middle of their sandwiches, it rises up and eats *them*. Very funny, eating your lunch on a squid's back. Why didn't they just name you squid?"

John didn't know what to say to that. And the notion of being eaten by a squid didn't seem awfully funny to him, but he smiled anyway and shrugged. The doughnuts had cheered Mr. Deener right up, and this was his way of making a joke.

Polly came back downstairs right then and said, "He's asleep."

Mr. Deener sighed very heavily.

Then Mrs. Barlow came in carrying a platter with a roast beef on it and potatoes and carrots heaped around. She laid it on a table set for all of them, Mrs. Barlow included, and with one plate at the head of the table where no one sat. It was clearly intended for 'the old man,' who was asleep upstairs. They waited only long enough to say grace, and then Mr. Deener plucked up a big serving spoon and began to shovel potatoes and slices of roast beef onto his plate, filling and filling and filling it until he could get nothing more onto it. Then he looked up, surprised, and said, "For you, my dear," and reached the plate across toward Polly, who shook her head politely.

"I couldn't eat half that much," she said. "*You* have it, Mr. Deener. You look thin."

"I *feel* thin, and that's the truth," Mr. Deener said. "I'm hungrier than two dogs." He winked at Danny and began immediately to eat, wrinkling up his forehead and chewing very steadily through the whole plate full of food, and then serving himself another, and then calling for pie when it was done, and for ice cream atop the pie and coffee to go with it, all of which Mrs. Barlow brought in great quantity, telling him fairly often that she had a mind to serve him dirt cutlets or worm sandwiches or some other awful thing if he didn't quit pigging the food up.

"He eats for two," Aunty Flo said, as if to explain Mr. Deener's tremendous appetite.

"I'm through," said Mr. Deener. "I'm full up." And he fed all the scraps to Ahab in a big heap. Then he said, "I'm going in to work," and he nodded to everyone, saying to John and Danny, "I'm building a device for the purposes of lunar exploration."

"A telescope?" asked Danny.

"No, a ladder," said Mr. Deener, and he strode out with his hands clasped across his stomach and a toothpick in his mouth.

"And you ought to go up to bed," said Aunty Flo to Polly. "You can show the boys to their room." Then she said to

58

John and Danny, "We'll get down to the business of helping you find your way home in the morning. Mr. Deener will see the way, if you'll help him to see it. We're all hoping that Mr. Deener will see the way."

"But . . ." John began, thinking that he would tell her about the spectacles and the window. They were still in his pocket, the spectacles were. He yawned, though, which is what interrupted his sentence. There was nothing to be done that night anyway. Things had turned out rather better than John had hoped. So they followed along up the stairs, passing the half-open door of the room where Mr. Deener worked.

He was dressed in an apron now, and had his hat off. He was twining holly leaves and ivy vines onto the rungs of a rope ladder. Heaped on the floor were old books and a ribby old umbrella with all the fabric pulled off and a scattering of globes made of coloured glass, like fishing floats, all of them the size of oranges.

Then they were past the door and up the second flight of stairs to the third floor, where yet another set of stairs wound up into a tower toward a fourth floor. It was a big house, and very mysterious, especially with the 'old man' sleeping up there somewhere, with his glazed doughnuts beside him on a plate.

It was a good house, though, with good people in it, and their bedroom was every bit as good as the rest of the house was. It had a fireplace of its own and was very cheerful with wood panelling and books and bright paintings on the wall of sailing ships and of two apes sitting in a tree, watching a crocodile go past on the ground below.

Danny fell asleep straightaway, but John lay awake for a time watching the fire burning low in the grate and Ahab asleep in front of it. The curtains were drawn back, and leaves drifted past it on the wind, maybe carrying hennypenny men. The sky was full of stars.

They had been lucky to fall among friends instead of among goblins. But John missed his bedroom and his mother and father. He knew they would think that he and Danny were lost, and that they wouldn't get any sleep that night at all. He wished that he could just call them on the telephone and tell them that he and Danny were safe, that they were spending the night at Aunty Flo's house and that Ahab was there with them.

But there wasn't any telephone. They were in a magical land, and there didn't seem to be any way home, despite what Aunty Flo had said about tomorrow. John started to think about all the mistakes he had made that day, of all the ways he had goofed up. He didn't want to think about them; he just did. It was his conscience, being rough on him. It had been a mistake to go climbing out of the window. It had been a mistake not to have told his parents. It had been a mistake to go meddling with magic spectacles in the first place.

It had been a mistake to run away that evening on the road and leave Danny to fight the goblins alone. Even though he had gone back, the truth was that he hadn't gone back fast enough. Would Danny have run away and left him? It didn't matter, did it? That's what his conscience told him. *Ahab* hadn't run off. Even a dog knew better than he did. He lay there thinking about all of these mistakes, and thinking that if a person never did anything at all, but just lay in bed asleep all the time, he wouldn't make nearly so many of them.

Thinking that way made him grow more and more sleepy and homesick until he began to dream about being home again and playing marbles in the backyard with Kimberly—or was it Polly? He dreamed that the back gate scraped open. It was Mr. Deener coming in, as if he lived there, as if it were *his* back yard. Only it wasn't Mr. Deener all of a sudden; it was a great fat goblin, wearing rats for shoes.

CHAPTER SEVEN

IN THE OLD HOUSE

There was a noise in the night, and it woke both of the boys up. It was a crash, like glass breaking, and then someone saying "Ow!" very loudly. Then it was quiet again.

"What was that?" asked Danny.

John sat up in bed and looked around. The fire in the fireplace had burned low, but the orange glow lighted the room well enough for them to see. Still, the room was spooky and full of shadows. "I don't know," John said. "Mr. Deener, maybe, making his ladder."

"To go to the moon? What does he mean by that?" Danny asked. "Why did he ask us if we'd come to help him? Do you think he wants the glasses?"

That was a surprising idea—one that John hadn't thought about. He climbed out of bed, found his jacket, and checked in the pocket. There were the spectacles, safe and sound. No one had stolen them in the night.

"The goblins want them," said Danny. "Maybe he wants them too. How do we know he doesn't?"

"I don't know, but I don't think he does. He seems too nice. And he likes doughnuts so well."

Neither one of them said anything for a moment, but just sat there, staring at the orange coals in the fireplace. John began thinking about people wanting to steal the glasses, and about Mr. Deener's moon ladder, and about the old man asleep upstairs. The thinking turned into worrying, and the worrying was worse because it was so

61

very late at night. Then all of a sudden Danny got up and stepped across to the door. He pushed it open softly. Light from the lamps in the hallway shined through into the room. He came back to his bed.

"Anybody out there?" asked John.

"No, but I could hear him working downstairs, dragging things around."

Now they weren't at all sleepy, and when Danny got up and started pulling his clothes on, John knew just what he was up to. "We'd better not," John said. "What if Polly or Aunty Flo wakes up and finds us messing around through the house? What are we going to tell them?"

"We're going to ask them how come they've got an old man held prisoner upstairs. He's a captive, is what I think. And he won't eat as long as they've got him locked up. He's on a hunger strike."

"A *hunger* strike," John said. "How do you know? It sounded to me like maybe he was sick or something—that he couldn't wake up long enough to eat."

But Danny was tying his shoes by then. He was getting ready to go out into the hallway. There was no stopping him; John could see that. Part of John wanted to go along. Part of him didn't. That had been the problem in the first place, when they had climbed through Mrs. Owlswick's window. That had been John's fault, mostly. He was the older brother. He should have been responsible. That's what had landed them here—his not being responsible. And this was another mistake—snooping around in an old house in the middle of the night when you were supposed to be in bed.

"Wait!" John called, "I'm going too," and Danny stopped by the door, peering through the crack again. John grabbed his pants and started to put them on, but he was moving slowly, because he still wasn't happy with the idea. He couldn't let his little brother go by himself, though, could he? What if something happened to him? John didn't want to be left alone either. He would go along with Danny in order to keep him out of trouble. He tied his shoes and put on his jacket.

The hallway was lit, but it was still shadowy and dim.

They walked along it toward the stairs. John listened to the quiet house. Even Mr. Deener had quit bumping around, maybe gone to bed. He couldn't hear anything at all except the rustling of leaves beyond the hallway windows, out in the windy night, and the creaking and cricking of the floorboards of the old house.

The stairs led up into the darkness of the tower. There were no lamps lit up there, and it was so gobliny and spooky that they stood at the bottom of the stairs for a moment and just looked at each other. Where would they go, up or down? Not up, certainly—not into the darkness.

"Wait," said Danny, as if he just then remembered something, and he sneaked back down the hall again, pushing into their bedroom. In a moment he was back with the candlestick that had sat by his bed. He gave it to John, and then struck a wooden match and lit it. Then he slipped the matches into his pocket, took his candle back, and stepped onto the stairs going up.

John followed. The light from the candle danced on the wall and threw their shadows back and forth across the old carpet. As the stairs wound around and up, the darkness closed up behind them, so that when they were halfway up the stairs they seemed suddenly to be in a dark closet. And then almost at once it got lighter, and there was the top landing and a round room opening out away from it. There were windows almost all the way around the room, so that you could see the dark countryside in every direction, lit by moonlight.

They stopped for a moment, there at the top of the stairs. John held onto Danny's shirt, to keep him from rushing in, or doing anything foolish. Outside the window, far below them, the dark forest fell away on two sides, running down along the meadow toward the ocean. The full moon shined in the sky like a hanging lantern, lighting up the meadow where the ghostly window hung above the pile of tree branches.

At least they *hoped* that the window still hung there. They couldn't see anything of it at all, not even the branches. Even with the moonlight it was too dark for that. Near where they thought the branches must be, a little way into the woods, there was the yellow glow of a fire burning—a goblin fire, maybe.

It was weird, that yellow glow in the black woods, but John didn't bother to wonder much about it because when he looked around the room he saw a bed, set against the wall and half hidden by a wide chair. Someone was lying in it—the old man. His face was hidden by the chair, and so he was shaded from the light of the candle. He stirred uneasily in his sleep.

John took a step backward, and then another one, feeling with his foot for the top tread of the stairs. It was wrong to be there, to be snooping in someone's room. The old man wasn't a prisoner. He wasn't locked in. There wasn't even a door on his room. John didn't dare breathe, and he would have blown out Danny's candle except that then it would be too dreadfully dark on the stairs. He turned and grabbed the railing and set out, jumping down the steps two at a time, halfway down before he stopped. Danny wasn't following again. He was staying in the room. He'll be caught, John thought, and there'll be trouble. Remembering their fight with the goblins on the road, John turned straight around and started back up.

"Danny!" John whispered, just as loud as he dared. There was no answer. He took three steps more, creeping along. "Daniel!" still no answer. There was nothing to do but to climb the rest of the stairs. When he did, there was Danny with his finger pressed to his lips. He motioned toward the other side of the room, wanting John to come along, to get a closer look at the man who lay in the bed. John shook his head.

Danny took a long, quiet step, stretching his neck to see past the edge of the big chair. He wanted a look at the face of the old man. John followed, grabbing a bit of Danny's shirt again and holding on, just in case something awful happened and he had to pull him away. They edged just a bit farther, into a circle of moonlight that glowed through the uncurtained window. They would just get a glimpse of the old man's face and be gone.

There were the doughnuts on a nightstand. He hadn't

taken a bite. There was a full water glass, too, and an unopened book.

He turned in his sleep, creaking the bedsprings. The boys froze there, half in the moonlight, still holding their candles. They squinted into the shadows. It was still too dim to see well. Before John could stop him, Danny raised his candlestick so that the candle light fell across the old man's face.

It was Mr. Deener.

In an instant, before John could snatch Danny away by the shirt, Danny turned and slammed into him, both boys tumbling back toward the stair well. Danny's candle fell off onto the rug and went out. Without bothering to pick it up, he dashed after his brother down the stairs, neither of them stopping until they had got to the bottom and had raced down the hall to their room.

"It couldn't have been," John whispered, without saying anything else first. He was out of breath. He took off his jacket and threw it on his bed.

"It *was*," said Danny. "I saw him straight on, when he turned. It was Mr. Deener. The old man is Mr. Deener!"

John sat down on his bed. Nothing made any sense. Why all the business about the 'old man' if the old man *was* really Mr. Deener? Was it all play acting? And hadn't Mr. Deener been at work downstairs? There! They could hear him again, whistling away in his workroom. "His twin brother!" John said. He must have a twin brother. Then, looking at Danny, he asked, "Where is your candle?"

"Dropped it."

"Upstairs? On the rug? What if they find it in the morning?"

Both of them went out the door and hurried back down the hall. They waited at the bottom landing, listening sharp to the sound of Mr. Deener's voice below. He was singing—the same ho, ho, ho song that he had sung on the road. It was him all right. They tip-toed up the stairs, one behind the other, John going first this time.

There the candle lay, right on the edge of the rug, in the moonlight. They crawled across the carpet toward it, so that if the man in bed awakened he wouldn't see them past the chair. Danny put his hand on the candle, and just then the man said, "What?" very loud, and rolled over heavily.

The boys dropped down flat on the floor. Danny pulled the candle out of the light. They didn't dare move, but lay there waiting for him to push himself up onto his elbows and look around. He didn't though. He began to breathe heavily and slowly. But just when it seemed safe and they started to crawl back toward the stairs, he said, "No!" as if he were talking to them.

John's eyes shot open, and he almost shouted out loud, but then he realized that the man was talking to someone in a dream.

"I didn't mean to," the sleeping Mr. Deener said. "I would have been there. I *should* have been there. But what could I . . ." He mumbled along, and the boys stayed there at the top of the stairs, lying half on the carpet, half on the wood floor, barely breathing until they heard him roll over again. He grew quiet, his breathing got heavy again, and ever so slowly and carefully the boys eased back down the stairs through the darkness, crawling down the first half backward, and then, when they could no long be seen from the room, they turned and slipped along as quickly as they could, back to their bedroom.

John pushed the door part way open and started to step through. Something stopped him: one of the tall bookcases near the fireplace had been swung away from the wall, like a door on hinges, and a dark passage opened beyond it. Someone had been in their room. Ahab slept by the fire as if nothing were wrong.

"Ssh!" John whispered, pointing toward the bookcase and the secret passage. But then a goblin popped up from behind Danny's bed, trying to put on Danny's jacket. The creature threw down the jacket, made the glasses sign at them, and then held his hand out. He had a round little head, bald on top, just like Mr. Deener's, and he wore the bat shirt and rat shoes and had a necklace of red jewels around his neck.

Just then John's jacket was jerked off his bed and was snatched underneath.

"Hey!" John shouted. Ahab woke up with a growl just as

66

John ran past Danny's bed, dropped down onto the floor, and shoved his hand in under his own bed. There was a coat sleeve, snaking away, and the face of a goblin looking out at him. He grabbed the sleeve and tugged, and the goblin that had it tugged back, and so John set his feet against the bed rail and hauled away on the sleeve, hauling out both the jacket and goblin.

"Goblins!" Danny shouted, loud enough to wake the house. Two or three more goblin faces appeared from out of the passage behind the bookcase, as if they thought Danny had called for them, and Ahab leaped up and ran at them. They jammed back into the darkness, cackling and gobbling and with Ahab chasing after, the whole crowd of them disappearing behind the bookcase.

The goblin in the red necklace hopped across the room toward Danny's knapsack, picking it up and dumping it out onto the floor. He snatched up a Tootsie Roll and shoved it into his mouth, looking very much like Mr. Deener, smacking down the candy like that.

"Ouch!" John shouted. He jerked his hand away and let go of his jacket. Two long lines of blood ran down his hand where the goblin had scratched him. The goblin scampered toward the passageway, carrying the jacket, with the spectacles in the pocket. John should have kept it on, and not left it lying on the bed, but he hadn't, and it was too late now.

But then just as the goblin ran into the darkness of the secret passage, Ahab ran out of it, barking and growling and chasing the goblin back into the room. John closed his eyes and hit the goblin just as hard as he could, which wasn't very hard, because the thing leaped up and swung the jacket at him, and John was just able to grab a handful of jacket cloth.

Danny's goblin rushed out through the door and away up the hallway, carrying the knapsack. So Danny jumped across to help John, and Ahab ran around them barking, and Mr. Deener slammed in out of the secret passage waving his soap gun.

"Leave off, boys!" he shouted.

John and Danny leaped away, as far as they could with

John still holding onto a jacket sleeve. 'Whoosh! Bang!' went the soap gun, and out came bubbles and fog and suds in a sort of pinky lather all over the goblin's head. It gave up straightaway and dropped the jacket. Then Mr. Deener swung the casement open on its hinge, pointed the gun at the goblin once again, and the creature climbed up onto the windowsill in a fright and flung itself out.

The boys rushed to the window. John was thinking that it was hard of Mr. Deener to force the goblin to jump out a third floor window. But just then there was a splash below, and the goblin was swimming across a pond in the moonlight, looking like shrunken, little Mr. Deener and making noises like a laughing turkey.

There was a shouting in the hall, and they turned to see Danny's goblin rushing back into the room, carrying a doughnut in either hand. He dashed straight toward the dark passageway, not looking to either side, and Aunty Flo ran into the room after him, carrying Danny's knapsack and waving a fireplace poker.

Mr. Deener shouldered his soap weapon to let go a blast, but it was too late. The little man was gone into the darkness, and Mr. Deener almost smacked into Aunty Flo as he ran out into the hallway. "I'll catch him down below!" shouted Mr. Deener. "I'll give him such a bath . . ."

The room fell quiet then, and they could hear Mr. Deener tromping heavily down the stairs. Aunty Flo stepped across and pulled a fat book out of the opened-up bookcase, and the case swung shut all by itself and settled into the wall. John took his jacket by the collar and gave it a shake, to straighten it out. It smelled like old fish, the jacket did, and a little like soap, and when he shook it, the spectacles slid out of the pocket onto the bed. John dropped the jacket over them to hide them, but it was too late.

"Was that Mr. Deener's doughnuts?" Danny asked.

Aunty Flo looked at the jacket, then at Danny. "Mr. Deener ate his doughnuts before supper," she said.

"I mean the old man's doughnuts, I guess," said Danny.

"Yes," said Aunty Flo. "Mr. Deener will want those spectacles." She said this to John, looking very serious.

"We need them," John said.

"We all need them, Mr. Deener especially. What I mean to say is that he mustn't be allowed to take them away by himself. Polly and I must be along, and Mrs. Barlow, too."

John sat down on his bed. This wasn't fair. What did *they* need the glasses for? They didn't have to get home. They *were* home. "We're lost," he said, and just for a moment it seemed like a good time to cry, if there ever was such a time, but he caught himself and swallowed hard and blinked his eyes clear.

"Hush," she said. "I know you are. We'll get you home, too, but to do it we've got to patch Mr. Deener back together again. It's very complicated, but I'll try to explain some of it to you in the morning."

They were interrupted when Mr. Deener's voice rang up from below. "I squirted the fellow down!" he shouted, tramping up into the hallway and heading down toward the room. "I caught him coming up out of the root cellar and I sudsed him right off. Demanded to see his fingernails. If I had a comb I could have made him entirely presentable." Mr. Deener laughed at the idea of making the goblin presentable, maybe dressing him in a coat and tie. Aunty Flo wasn't so cheerful, though.

"You oughtn't to have left the door to the root cellar unlocked, Mr. Deener. Especially not after you knew that the goblins were out on the road tonight."

Mr. Deener looked very sad all of a sudden. "Don't tell Miss Polly," he said.

Aunty Flo shook her head. "I won't. The girl's asleep, but . . . What on earth!" She snatched up John's hand to look at the scratches that the goblin had given him. They weren't deep, but they looked raggedy and awful. "The soap, Mr. Deener."

"Poor Miss Polly," said Mr. Deener, shaking his head.

"Miss Polly is sleeping very happily. Fetch the goblin soap, Mr. Deener."

Mr. Deener shook his head again. He wasn't listening. "My idea," he said out loud, but to no one, "is to soap them clean. Wash them off. Make them respectable. Anything can be made respectable if you clean it up with a bit of soap."

69

"Bother the goblins, Mr. Deener! Come along, John, and we'll fetch the soap together if Mr. Deener won't help."

Mr. Deener brightened up just then and said, "If it's soaping needs to be done, then I'm the man, aren't I? You would be John?" he asked, and he set out toward the door, motioning for John to come along.

John looked at his jacket, and then at Aunty Flo, who winked at him, and he turned around to follow Mr. Deener, who said, as they were walking down toward the stairs, "I'm certain the little men didn't *mean* to scratch you. They get into trouble easily enough, but they don't mean anything by it, if you understand me. You mustn't be too hard on them."

Looking down at the scratches on his arm, John *didn't* quite understand. What he did see was how curious it was that Mr. Deener looked so entirely like an overgrown goblin that had been fattened and neatened. Muss his hair, though, and put rats on his feet . . .

CHAPTER EIGHT

MR. DEENER'S GLASS MAGIC

Mr. Deener led John into his workroom. He looked around, as if he were surprised at the mess, and said, "Tut, tut." There was the rope ladder, lying in the middle of the floor, tangled up with vines. Swept against the wall was a pile of broken glass and a lot of leaves and twigs and trash. Dozens of drawings and maps and pictures hung on the walls everyplace that there weren't shelves covered with bottles and bottles and bottles of coloured glass chips. Some of the bottles were full of chips of a single colour—red or blue or purple or green. Some were a sort of circus of chips, every colour on earth all mixed in together.

John thought at once of the fishbowl full of marbles that they had bought from the little man in the Plaza, and of the glass in Mrs. Owlswick's window, and then of the henny-penny men, out on the meadow, carrying their little heaps of glass chips. They had pretty clearly been flying them to Mr. Deener, for him to put in his bottles.

A great, iron-bound chest lay on the floor in a corner, full of heaps of rhinestone jewelry—bracelets and pins and necklaces and rings and belt buckles and buttons and odds and ends, and straightaway John thought of Kimberly with her goblin treasure and of the goblin in the woods with the jewelled Christmas tree on his bat vest and of the jacket-stealing goblins in the room tonight with their rings and necklaces.

Stacked against the walls were windows of stained and

71

leaded glass, looking very much like Mrs. Owlswick's window. Like the glass chips in the bottles, the glass in the windows was of many colours, washed-out like colours in moonlight. Somehow these windows didn't look as if they were meant to be used in a house. They had some other, maybe magical purpose.

There was other stuff lying about the room too, but John didn't get much of a glimpse at it because Mr. Deener had found the soap. It was on a washstand, by a pitcher of water and a bowl.

"Let me see that wound, then," said Mr. Deener. "I'm terribly sorry about this. Awfully sorry. Why does this sort of thing always happen to *me?*"

It *hadn't* happened to him, of course, but John didn't say so. Mr. Deener seemed too upset for John to say anything. Pulling his glasses down his nose and squinting at the scratches, Mr. Deener said, "I don't *want* them to carry on so, but they won't listen to me." He slathered pink soap onto John's hand and then rinsed it off with water from the pitcher. John expected it to sting, but it didn't; it merely itched. "There we are, good as new. Or very nearly."

Sure enough, the scratches were gone. There was nothing left but two reddish marks that ran along the back of his hand, as if they were left over from scratches he had gotten years before. "I really am sorry," said Mr. Deener. "How can I make it up to you? I'm not a *bad* man. No worse than most. People *think* I am, maybe. I can't stand people thinking that about me, that's all. It makes me so awfully mortified."

"Make it up to me?" asked John, puzzled. "It's not *your* fault." Then he remembered that it had been Mr. Deener who had left the cellar door open. Maybe that's what he was talking about.

Mr. Deener soaped his own hands and lathered them up. Then he soaped them again, rinsed them and soaped them again, working away at them. "Never clean enough," he said. "Of course they think badly of me. I did it on purpose. She knows that, too, but she won't say so. She's too good. Too good. I've done any number of bad things since it happened."

72

"Since you left the cellar door open?" asked John, wondering if he hadn't ought to get back to the bedroom. Maybe there were more goblins getting in right then, through windows left open or something.

"Not the door, no." He set about washing his hands again, looking very sorrowful.

Something was odd about Mr. Deener. *Lots* of things were odd about Mr. Deener. John thought for a moment and then said, "The goblin got the old man's doughnuts, I guess."

"Alas!" said Mr. Deener. "The thief steals from himself!" And he began to wash his hands again furiously, although he had already dried them once. "I'll have a doughnut myself. Just one. I mean three. Mrs. Barlow will be beastly to me in the morning, but I don't care. Everyone is beastly to me. I'm shabbily treated, but I can't say so. I'm the saddest man alive."

With that Mr. Deener started to cry in big, humping sorts of sobs, washing and washing at his hands and slopping soapy water all over the floor. "I can't wash it out!" he cried finally, and he flung open the curtain across a pair of big windows with his soapy hands.

The moon shined through onto the floor, and Mr. Deener stepped into its light and peered out through the glass, still crying and shaking his wet hands. He made a rush for the soap and water again, but stopped himself and said, "It's no good!" Then he stepped across to where the glass windows lay in their frames, leaning against the wall. He sorted through them, one by one, humming very loudly, although the song he hummed had no tune to it; it was just a mess of sounds.

John moved backward toward the door. Mr. Deener seemed to have gone crazy, with all his hand washing and humming. Half of John wanted to run, but the other half wanted to see what Mr. Deener would do. He was up to something, some sort of inventing, maybe.

Mr. Deener pushed a window out from among the others. It was as tall as his head, very heavy, and dark blue, like the sky at nightfall. He pulled it into the centre of the floor and set it into a little wooden stand in the moonlight.

Then, without stopping even for a moment, and all the time crying and shaking his head, he stepped across to where the jars of glass chips sat and found a jar full of light blue chips, like the sky at afternoon.

Then he picked up a skinny little table, like a plant stand, set it in front of the window, and set the jar of chips on the stand. He bent over the chest full of jewelry, humming loudly now and sort of singing, and stirred things up with his hands until he found a big, round piece of glass, like a paperweight. It was muddy brown, and there was a face carved on it which might have been his own face. John was too far off to see.

John stood in the doorway now, ready to run away up the stairs. There was something horrible about magic, and about the way that Mr. Deener seemed to have forgotten him standing there. He seemed, in fact, to have forgotten himself or to have lost himself. John took a step back, holding onto the door frame, so that only his head was in the room. Mr. Deener didn't seem to be Mr. Deener any more. He was something less now—the ghost or the dream of someone.

Mr. Deener threw open the window just then, BANG, with a crash. The wind blew into the room, throwing leaves across the floor in the moonlight. He stood in the wind, pulling on a thick rope that hung from the ceiling. One end of the rope had a hook on it, and Mr. Deener shoved the hook through a hole in the window frame. His hair blew in the wind, and he still hummed his little song. He looked straight at John, but didn't seem to see him, as if Mr. Deener had quite simply lost his mind.

He jerked a second rope, and down fell a long, curly ivy vine, with the leaves still green on it. The end of it was laced into a round basket, and into this basket he slipped the glass ball with the face on it, and then pulled it, too, up into the light. The moon shined into the room, straight through the night-blue window, swirling around like water going down a sink. It swirled into the jar of glass chips and then shot straight through into the glass ball wrapped in ivy vine. John could see the light move through the glass like water through a tube. Mr. Deener stood right behind it, quiet now. He was no longer humming or singing or crying or talking to himself. The moonlight flew into his face, so that from behind him, from where John stood in the doorway watching, the back of his head was dark, with a ring of wild, coloured moonlight spinning around it.

And then a goblin stood next to Mr. Deener.

It was half Mr. Deener's size. It was ugly and skinnier, too—a sort of shrivelled-up Mr. Deener. It shook its head and gobbled a little bit, as if trying out its voice for the first time. Then it began to cry, sounding very much as Mr. Deener had sounded just a few minutes earlier. Finally, gobbling and cackling and crying, it ran toward the open window and climbed out into the night, off to look for a vest and a pair of rat shoes, maybe. Running along behind it was a mouse. Only it couldn't be a mouse, because it ran on its hind legs. In a moment it had gone outside, too, and disappeared into the darkness.

The wind slammed the window shut. The moon disappeared behind a cloud. Mr. Deener sat down on the wooden floor and scratched his head, and then sighed. He stood up, latched the window, put the bits and pieces of his magic away, and then seemed to see John for the first time.

"Why you've come after all!" he cried, and he began to whistle very merrily.

"What was that?" asked John, closing his mouth, which until then had been open wide, like the mouth of a codfish. He didn't dare come back into the room, but he didn't want to leave quite yet, either. He wanted to know what it was he had seen.

"That was self pity," said Mr. Deener. "Gone now, along with the rest of them. I've come upon some magic that I use to chase off all the little demons in me, all the botherations. I'm full of botherations. Nobody's got as many of them as I have. It's really very easy, just a matter of reflected light. It works when soap won't, which is most of the time."

"Are all the goblins . . .?" John began.

And Mr. Deener interrupted him, as if he didn't want him to finish the sentence. "Yes, they are. All little bits of me—a couple of dozen, I should think. I've gotten rid of the ones that hurt the most. Sometimes I've got to make two or

75

three goblins to do it right, because my feelings run very deep. Soon I shall forget that I ever had this last one. That's the beauty of it. Once they're gone, they're gone for good. It's a matter of making yourself small—so small that things can't get at you."

"Unless someone leaves the root cellar unlocked," John said.

Mr. Deener looked at him curiously. "That's a different matter, isn't it? They do like to come sneaking back in to steal things. It breaks you to pieces, of course, turning bits of yourself into goblins this way. But there are many parts of us that we would rather not have, aren't there?"

Yes, there were. That's what John thought. He didn't say so, though. He had thought that Mr. Deener was simple-minded, and here he was, talking very deep. Again he wondered—how many Mr. Deeners were there? He decided to take a chance. "Is that you asleep upstairs?"

"We'll *both* get a doughnut," said Mr. Deener, brightening up, but ignoring John's question. "Then Mrs. Barlow shan't get mad and say she's going to feed me clods. She won't be mad at *you*. It wouldn't be hospitable. And if she's not mad at you for hooking a doughnut, then she can't be mad at me either. That wouldn't be fair." He was cheerful again. "I'm really very fond of Mrs. Barlow. If I were a younger man . . ." He began to look wistful and sad again, and all of a sudden he rushed off, after a doughnut.

He went straight past John, toward the stairs that led down to the living room and off toward the kitchen. He was whistling merrily now, and his eyes were pleasant and silly, as they had been at dinner last night. "Which of the brothers are you again?" he asked over his shoulder and up the stairs.

He got no answer, though, for John had run off in the other direction, toward the third floor. He shouted "Goodnight," from the next landing, so that Mr. Deener wouldn't think him impolite. It was too late for doughnuts and too late for magic, and very nearly too late for politeness. Again he thought that there were parts of himself that might easily be turned into goblins, but somehow the idea of it wasn't a good one. It might have

been a good one yesterday, maybe even an hour ago. But right now it seemed to him that Mr. Deener had made a mistake, maybe a lot of them. That's what the goblins were—a lot of little mistakes wearing rat shoes.

What John wanted to do was find Danny and Ahab and the broken spectacles. He wanted to fall asleep, and wake up back on Pine Street in Orange, and find out that he had been having a long and frightening dream.

CHAPTER NINE

THE MYSTERY OF MR. DEENER

"Mr. Deener is sleeping late," said Aunty Flo, passing the pancake syrup to Danny. "He's had a hard night. Nights are the worst for him. During the day he hasn't so many temptations. But at night he begins to worry about things. And if there's any mischief that he means to do, he'll do that at night too."

John thought that the same thing was true about himself. It was at night that he did most of his worrying. "I saw him turn into a goblin last night," he said to Aunty Flo. He had already told Danny all about it, when he had got back to his room, and the two had fallen asleep finally very early in the morning. Polly had knocked on their door at ten, to tell them that Mrs. Barlow had made waffles, and John had waked up to find that it hadn't been a dream at all, that they were still lost in the magical land and were no closer to home now than they had been yesterday.

Ahab put his head in Danny's lap and looked at him, and so Danny said, "Can we feed Ahab at the table?"

"As quickly as we can," said Aunty Flo, tearing off a bit of waffle and offering it to the dog. She sat still for a moment, and then said, very seriously, "Mr. Deener is a broken man. I don't mean that his spirit is broken, or that he's a sad man, but that he has broken himself in half. And now he thinks that by using his inventions he can break off little parts of what is left of himself that he doesn't like."

"Do you mean," asked Danny, "that he can just forget bad things that he did?"

"Not that he *did*, so much," said Aunty Flo, "but what he *is*. None of us are as good as we should be, are we?"

John nodded. He knew that was true.

"And yet there's something very good in us that makes us feel bad about not being as all-together good as we would like to be."

She was getting confusing, and yet John knew just what she meant. She was talking about a conscience, of course. And lately John had been a little too bothered by his.

"She means a conscience," said Polly—just what John had been thinking. "Mr. Deener's conscience has gotten all swelled up because of something that he thinks he did. He used to say that it beat him with sticks, and there wasn't a moment in the day when he wasn't crying because his conscience was beating him and beating him with sticks."

"*I'll* beat him with sticks," said Mrs. Barlow, coming into the room just then and laying down a bowl of milk for Ahab. "He's gone and pinched all the doughnuts. He must have eaten two dozen last night." She looked very fierce, and was shaking the wooden dowel that she strung the glazed doughnuts on. "I have half a mind to give him a good whack. That's what he needs—a bonk on the conk. All this crying and moaning ought to be . . ."

But she didn't say what it ought to be; she whacked the stick into her hand a couple of times and then said, "Now I've got to make more, I guess."

"It's my fault," said John. "I was with him last night when he was feeling especially bad for having left the cellar door open, and I told him that doughnuts might make him feel better." That wasn't really true, but Mrs. Barlow got less fierce when he said it, so it had a good result.

"Well," she said, nodding at John, "that's a different case, isn't it? I won't thrash him today, then. But he'd better not come bothering me for more doughnuts before dinnertime, or I'll give him a doughnut in the eye. See if I don't."

"Anyway," Aunty Flo said, going on, "Mr. Deener's conscience won't let him rest. A little bit of conscience

pushes us along to try to do better; too much of it, though
. . ." She thought for a moment, trying to find the right
word. "Too much of it *paralyzes* us. Do you know what I
mean?"

"She means it doesn't help anymore," said Polly. "Mr.
Deener sits in a slump all day sometimes. Nothing is any
good for. Everything is bad or sad or some other awful
thing. That's what too much conscience did to Mr. Deener.
So we're taking care of him, hoping that he can put himself
right. We're all going to help him patch himself up."

"How can we patch him up," John asked, "when he keeps
taking himself apart?"

Aunty Flo shrugged. "That's the problem, isn't it? He's
got to *want* to be patched up."

"Is that the other half of him upstairs?" asked Danny.

Aunty Flo nodded. "That's the half of him that can't bear
to think. So he sleeps the day and night out. And if he does
awaken for a moment, he's blind. He's not really blind, but
has made himself blind, because there are things that he
doesn't want to see."

"It's terribly sad," said Polly. "Because really he's such a
nice man, but he doesn't know that."

"It's easy for us to know that about others," said Aunty
Flo, "but hard to know that about ourselves."

"Why does he eat so many doughnuts?" John asked,
helping himself to another waffle.

Polly passed him the syrup. "He likes them. You've got to
like *something* or all of you might as well be asleep."

"So the goblins," said Aunty Flo, "are all little bits of Mr.
Deener that he's got rid of by glass magic. One by one he's
cast out his grouchinesses and regrets and—what was it
that he got rid of last night?"

"Self pity," said John. "That's what he called it, anyway.
It looked a lot like him, too."

Aunty Flo nodded as if this didn't surprise her. "I should
think that it *would* look very much like him. All of his
goblins do in this way and that way. Some of them, though,
the worst ones, are shrivelled up and bent and rather
awful. And I'm afraid that left alone, without Mr. Deener's
conscience to keep them in line, they can do a powerful lot

81

of mischief. They're getting worse, and the worse they get, the more downcast Mr. Deener becomes."

"Yes," said Polly. "All his glass magic doesn't seem to help. It seems to make him worse. It's like every time a little bad part of him turns into a goblin and runs off into the woods, a good part of him goes along with it."

"The henny-penny men!" said John. So it hadn't been a mouse that had run out after the goblin last night.

"That's right, the leaf men," said Polly.

Now John *was* confused. "But they bring him the glass chips. If the glass magic is so awful, why do they fill his glass jars?"

"Who said it was awful?" asked Aunty Flo. "It brought you two to us, didn't it? And it will take you both home again, too. Mr. Deener has found a way to put a good thing to bad uses. He knows it, too, and that bothers him no end and makes things worse."

"But what I want to know," said Danny, "is about the Mr. Deener upstairs. What did he . . .?" Just then Aunty Flo put her finger to her lips and hushed him. Mr. Deener himself was coming along, down the hallway, singing a song about waffles.

Mrs. Barlow came back out of the kitchen and gave him a look, as if to let him know that she knew about his eating all the doughnuts in the house, and when he sat down in front of his empty plate and winked everyone a good morning with either eye, Mrs. Barlow set one little corner of waffle on the plate. It was a piece about as big as a shirt pocket. Then she lay the rest of the waffles one by one on the rest of the plates and said, "There's *one* of us that shouldn't be very hungry, I should think."

But Mr. Deener's face looked so fearfully sad all of a sudden that Danny said, "I'm full, actually," and he speared up his own waffle with a fork and dropped it onto Mr. Deener's plate.

"You can have mine too," said John, although in truth John would have liked to eat it himself.

"Neither one of you will regret it, my good fellows," said Mr. Deener, hacking the waffles into pieces and dropping gobs of butter onto them. "You're good men, both of you.

82

I'm going to turn you into something nice with one of my inventions."

John and Danny looked at each other, startled just a little bit. But Aunty Flo shook her head at them, with a look on her face that seemed to say that Mr. Deener was only talking through his hat—that he meant well and that they needn't be alarmed. Then she nodded at John and made the glasses sign with her fingers, and John took the magic spectacles out of his pocket and laid them on the table.

Mr. Deener put his fork down and stared at the spectacles. Then, very slowly, he turned them over. Then he put his finger through the rim of the missing lens, as if to make sure that it wasn't just very clear glass. He picked the spectacles up and looked through the good lens. His eye seemed suddenly to be as big around as the moon. "Superior glass," he said. "Very superior glass. Don't see much of it these days."

"What we need to know, Mr. Deener," said Aunty Flo, "is can you repair these broken spectacles?"

Mr. Deener sat there for a moment, staring through the green glass. Then he said, "Altogether too dangerous," and shoved a fork full of waffle into his mouth.

Aunty Flo reached down and patted him on the arm. "You're just the man for it, Mr. Deener. I was just telling the boys that if there is one thing Mr. Deener *doesn't* mind, it's a bit of danger."

Mr. Deener pretended not to hear her.

"These boys have got to get home. They've been telling me about a magic window out on the meadow, and that they've got to climb through it, back into their own house. Only they can't see the window, because their glasses are broken."

"*I'm* not the one that's got to get them home, surely," said Mr. Deener. "Why must it be me?" He looked mad all of a sudden. Here was a new Mr. Deener again. Only it wasn't just a mad Mr. Deener; the anger was mixed up with fear and a couple of other things.

"You know why it must be you," said Aunty Flo. "We've all been waiting for it to be you."

"Let's go out on the meadow this morning," Polly said,

83

"and find their window. I'd like to see their house, too."

"Well," Mr. Deener grumbled, "I *could* find their blasted window for them, I suppose." Then he cheered up suddenly, slipped the spectacles into his coat pocket, and said, "I've got an idea! Bother your window. We don't need windows. You two can come along home on my moon ladder. It will get you to where you want to go just as surely as these glasses will. I'm certain of it. And it will be altogether more pleasant."

Aunty Flo had got up from the table and now stood behind Mr. Deener. She slid her hand into his coat pocket and took the glasses out.

"I'll need those," he said.

"And you can have them when you're ready to have them. Right now they belong to the boys."

Polly stood up and headed for the kitchen. "I'll just help Mrs. Barlow pack a picnic lunch for the meadow," she said.

"But my moon ladder!" Mr. Deener said.

Everybody was gone, though. Aunty Flo, John, and Danny went off upstairs, and Polly to the kitchen. Only Ahab was left sitting by Mr. Deener's chair, helping him eat pieces of waffle. Mr. Deener slumped down lower and lower, jamming his chin into his chest and squinting up his eyes until his face looked smashed. He sat that way while the rest of his waffles got cold.

CHAPTER TEN

THE FOUNTAIN IN THE WOODS

From the top of the hill they could see far and wide, down toward the meadow and the sea and up toward where the meadow turned into hills and the hills into mountains until all of it was lost in the misty distances. They couldn't see how far the forest stretched, because they were too close to it to see anything but trees.

The strange thing was that the land seemed to be half in summer and half in winter, or maybe autumn. The hills were brown and dry, and the sycamore trees were almost leafless. The dry grass ran out onto the meadow, a mile or more up beyond the house, and then got a little greener and a little greener until, very near to the house itself, it was all so very green that it seemed as if even the coldest winter or driest summer couldn't wither it.

There was a broad stream, almost a river, that ran along out of the brown hills, but it had only a muddy trickle of water in it, so that it soaked into the ground and disappeared before it even got to the meadow. Where it dropped toward the ocean, the river-bed was as dry as old stones.

Right around the house, though, the trees were leafy green and were thick and dark. Wildflowers grew at the edge of the woods, and the little stream that the boys had first seen from their bedroom window rushed along merrily, in and out of the trees.

Danny said that maybe there had been a fire that had

burned off half of everything they could see. But Aunty Flo said that actually there hadn't been any fire—the land was just half asleep. Mr. Deener began whistling a song very loud just when she said this, and he began to have all sorts of trouble with the stuff he'd brought along in his basket, nearly dropping it all onto the ground.

There were two bottles of glass chips and a round glass lens as big as a plate, which he said was made of something called isinglass. There was a chunk of green cheese, with holes in it, and jars of cold mint tea, of pond water, and of grass clippings floating in morning dew. There were three china saucers that Mr. Deener had borrowed from Mrs. Barlow, which were so thin and delicate that if you held one up to your eye you could see the green shadows of trees and grass moving through the white porcelain. He had it all in baskets, along with their food, and the soap gun and a pruning clippers.

As they tramped along, John and Danny kept watching the woods, looking for goblins. They knew that Ahab would smell the little men and bark if any came around, but they watched for them anyway. Aunty Flo had said that the goblins wouldn't come out into the sunlight. But they could see that there was a fog lying in the woods, and if the fog came out onto the meadow and hid the sun . . . Maybe the goblins wouldn't bother with them if Mr. Deener was there with the soap gun. John patted his jacket pocket to make sure the spectacles were safe. He wished that he had something better to do with them than carry them around, but he didn't.

They were down onto the meadow, almost to where the brush was piled up, when the first of the henny-penny men flew past on his leaf. A dozen more followed. They circled around Mr. Deener's head, and one even landed on his shoulder and said something in his ear. Then it sat there on its leaf, riding on Mr. Deener's shoulder as they cut along across the meadow. Mr. Deener didn't look very happy all of a sudden, and he scrunched up his neck, as if the little man were tickling him.

There was the pile of brush just ahead. They could see it plainly now, and of course there was no window above it,

not that they could see anyway. John and Danny and Ahab ran toward it. Ahab sniffed around, wagging his tail, then put his paws on one of the limbs as if he thought he could climb up and through the window. He barked twice, and his barking was loud on the quiet meadow. For a moment John thought that he *would* climb through, that maybe Ahab saw the window even though none of the rest of them could. But then the pile of limbs slid apart and Ahab tumbled off into the grass, and John was left with the sad feeling that Ahab had seen something that he couldn't quite find his way to—maybe their father and mother or maybe just their bedroom.

Mr. Deener set down all the stuff and went off to the edge of the woods with the pruning clippers. He hacked off a few sprigs of oak leaves and brought them back across to lay them on the brush heap. There were three henny-pennies bothering him now, one on his shoulder and two flying around his head on sycamore leaves. They were chattering at him in tiny voices. Mr. Deener frowned. He seemed put out, like a child being yelled at by its mother.

He nodded his head and then shook his head and then said, "All right! I will!" and swatted at one of the henny-pennies as if it were a bug. The leaf dipped on the wind, sliding under his hand. Then it swooped back in and the little man on it began to talk into Mr. Deener's ear again.

Two more henny-pennies flew past John and Danny. They looked amazingly like Mr. Deener too, except maybe a little handsomer—not quite gone to fat yet and with more hair. And they were dressed pretty elegantly, too. John wondered where the little men got their clothes, and then he remembered how Polly had been sitting by the fire, sewing up doll costumes.

"Here, you boys!" hollered Mr. Deener. They ran to where he stood, Ahab following along. Polly and Aunty Flo were a ways off, picking wildflowers. "Take this," said Mr. Deener to John, handing him a jar full of rose-pink glass chips. "Now stand over that way. No. Farther. Three more steps." John stepped backwards. He was about thirty feet away from Mr. Deener and about the same distance from the window, or at least from where the window was supposed to be.

"Now you," said Mr. Deener to Danny. "*You* take this jar, and stand over there." And he pointed off a ways, in the other direction, so that Danny ended up thirty feet to the other side of the pile of brush, straight across from where John stood. His jar was full of leaf-green glass chips. Mr. Deener walked back and forth, still bothered by the henny-pennies flying around his head. There were ten or twelve of them watching him now, giving him advice. They stayed pretty clear, though, as if they approved of what he was doing, and didn't want to get in the way.

But just then Mr. Deener laid the isinglass lens back in the basket, and said, "It's lunch time! Isn't it?" And all of sudden the henny-pennies swarmed around his head, zig-zagging in and out, yammering at him, and he began to shout "Okay! Okay! I *will* do it, too. And it'll be the end of me. The end of poor Mr. Deener!"

Polly came running up and shooed the henny-penny men away. She put a wildflower through the collar of Mr. Deener's coat and gave him a kiss on the cheek and said he was a dear man.

"Am I?" he asked, sniffing.

"You certainly are," she said. "The leaf men are just trying to help you, though."

"Why won't they quit *lecturing* me?" he asked. "Why must they always hound me? It's because they think I'm a slacker. I'll show them, though."

"Of course you will, Mr. Deener," Polly said. "You'll just show them and show them and show them. Look." She bent over and moved things around in one of the baskets, finding a glazed doughnut under the cloth covering. "For you," she said. "Mrs. Barlow packed them. Nevermind what she said this morning. We don't have many, though, so you mustn't eat them all at once."

"One will give me strength," he said. Then he winked at Polly. "Mrs. Barlow is sweet on me, I think. She always has a doughnut ready. She can be awful when she doesn't understand me. But then, like magic, there she is with a doughnut. I might just ask Mrs. Barlow to . . . Imagine, having a woman like that to cook for you. Doughnuts at all hours of the day . . ."

Polly gave him the doughnut, but when he started to take a bite, in flew the henny-pennies, around and around his head, trying to land on the doughnut. One snatched a hunk of doughnut as it flew past on its leaf, and began to eat, holding the bit of doughnut in both hands.

"Here!" shouted Polly, starting to laugh, and she pulled out a teacup filled with what looked like little bitty doughnuts, and the henny-penny men swarmed around her for a moment, helping themselves until she put the teacup back into the basket.

Aunty Flo came up just then. "Take the jar from John," she said to Polly. "And I'll take Danny's." Then to Mr. Deener she said, "The boys can't hold the jars, Mr. Deener. They've got to see through the lens. We're going to show them their bedroom window. They can't see the window if they're holding onto the jars, can they?"

"Ah," said Mr. Deener, licking his fingers. "Then we'll need some forked sticks."

Polly and Aunty Flo took the jars, and John and Danny ran around finding forked sticks—twelve of them. Mr. Deener took the sticks and jammed them down into the soft ground, two together, with their forks pointing into the air. Then he shoved two more into the ground a few feet behind the first two, and two more behind those, and then he balanced one of Mrs. Barlow's china saucers in each pair of forks so that the saucers, finally, stood one behind the other in a row, each of them about a foot above the meadow grasses.

"Now for the mirrors," he said, "and then the pond water and the morning dew," and he hurried across to plant more sticks, peering up at the sun and then again at the moon, which was high in the sky even though it was the middle of the morning. He balanced little round mirrors on each new pair of sticks, so that the mirrors pointed at the jars full of glass chips and at the plates and at the moon.

Then he upended two of the baskets and set the pond water and the grassy dew on each of them. He found a big rock and set the mint tea on it, making sure that the tea and the pondwater and the dew were in line, straight across from the three china saucers. Then, at last, he lay the smelly piece of cheese behind the tea and stood back to have a look at all of it. Motioning at John and Danny to follow him, he walked a good ways off toward the woods carrying the isinglass lens and one last pair of forked sticks.

"We'll use the rays of the moon," he said very seriously. "Glass magic always requires the moon. It's all a matter of reflection, of seeing the inside out of things. The moon shines here all the time. It's always full, stuck right up there in the sky. Here, hold this lens while I set the sticks."

In a moment everything was ready, or seemed to be. The saucers and pond water and all the rest was spread around the meadow. Polly and Aunty Flo held their jars up so that sunlight shined through them. The curved sides of the jars took the light and beamed it toward the mirrors, where it bounced back and forth, cutting this way and that way and right through the three china saucers, where it seemed to get lost. But it wasn't lost; it was just very pale and seemed to be moving slowly under where the window hung. It looked as if the pile of brushwood was floating in a pale green bath. From there the light moved through the oak leaves atop the brush, across the meadow flowers and through the dew and the pondwater and the tea and through the holes in the green cheese, and made the big isinglass lens shine as if it stood in an ocean tidepool on a sunny day.

"Have a look," said Mr. Deener.

John went first. He bent over in front of the lens and squinted up his eyes. The isinglass wasn't clear. It was full of tiny lines like cracks in ice. But through it, floating over the meadow and the heap of brush was. . .Well, it wasn't the window, exactly. John couldn't quite make it out.

Just then a cloud passed across the sun and the meadow fell into cloud shadow. The picture through the lens grew clearer. It was the window frame, just the bottom part of it. The shadow helped. Too much sun was no good.

"Here," said Danny. "Let me see."

John moved and Danny took his place. He looked

through the lens for a moment before saying, "There's a bit of it, anyway."

Now it was Mr. Deener's turn. He looked through the lens and then stood up. He frowned. "This isn't right," he said, and he stepped away again and looked over the meadow. "Lower your jar an inch!" he yelled at Aunty Flo. Then he looked across the top of his thumb and moved his hand to follow the light as it angled across the meadow. "We need a secondary lens," he said. Then he shrugged and put his hands in his pockets. "The whole experiment is worthless without a secondary lens. *This* isn't going to do the job. We might as well eat."

"Perhaps this will help," John said, pulling the spectacles out of his pocket.

Mr. Deener tilted backward, very nearly falling over. "No," he said. "Those won't work. Those aren't worth a nickel. Might as well let the dog wear them. Throw them away, that's my advice. Pitch them into the woods. They're trouble for all of us. We'll use my moon ladder tonight and be home by dawn. We don't need a pair of broken spectacles."

There was a flurry of sycamore leaves in the air just then, and a dozen or more henny-penny men looped crazily around Mr. Deener's head. They hollered at him, seeming to be very mad about something. One of them pinched his nose and another tugged on his ear and then yelled straight into it. But their hollering sounded more like singing than hollering, and John couldn't make out a word of it.

There came a shout from the direction of Aunty Flo just then: "What are you telling them, Mr. Deener?" she called.

He dodged away from the henny-pennies and then looked up, seeming very guilty. "Nothing!" he shouted back. "Only that we'll need a secondary lens. This one alone isn't a proper filter!" Then he stood thinking, but he wouldn't look at the broken spectacles in John's hand. "I've got it!" he said, and tramped away toward the picnic baskets. The henny-pennies followed along, keeping watch, as if they were suspicious that Mr. Deener might try some trick or another, some bit of mischief.

John and Danny went along too. "It's a doughnut that we

need," said Mr. Deener, and he bent over to fish around in the basket. "Hey!" he cried, pulling the cloth completely away from the top. "What's this!" He pulled out a half-eaten doughnut. Something had been nibbling at it, all around the edge. There was the sound of something messing around among the cups and saucers.

"Mice!" shouted Danny, as if he was happy with the idea of mice riding in the picnic basket. Ahab barked. Aunty Flo came running up, carrying her jar.

Mr. Deener reached in and pulled out the cups and saucers, and there, hiding among them, were two henny-penny men. Their leaves lay on the bottom of the basket, and on each of the leaves lay a heap of doughnut bits. "Thieves!" cried Mr. Deener, feeding Ahab what was left of the doughnut that the little men had been working at.

Polly helped the henny-pennies out of the basket along with their leaves. She piled three or four of the little doughnuts into their arms, and the heavy leaves wobbled away in the breeze with Ahab running along below. One of them threw a tiny doughnut for Ahab to catch. Then they flew into the shadows of the woods and were gone.

Ahab stood at the edge for a moment, next to the stream, sort of sniffing the air. Then, suddenly, he walked backward, very slowly and with his tail stretched out straight and the hair along his back standing up.

John saw that something was wrong even before Ahab started to bark. The fog had drifted to the very edge of the woods. "Goblins!" John shouted, and then came the barking, and all of them were running toward the trees. Mr. Deener stopped long enough to pick up his soap gun. But he was a little slow, and by the time he came puffing up to where the rest of them stood, there wasn't a goblin to be seen, but only the sound of goblin laughter way off in the foggy darkness of the oak woods.

"Look here!" cried Danny, and he pointed to where a piece of rhinestone jewelry lay half buried in the dirt. "Goblin treasure," he said.

"That's just what it is," said Mr. Deener, picking up the piece and taking a look. He tilted his glasses up and peered at it closely, turning it over in his hand. "They were going to wreck the lens, is what I think." He pointed to where the lens stood in its forked sticks, almost among the trees. "The little leaf men happened along and . . ."

And right then Polly shouted, and all of them ran to where she crouched on her knees in the leaves. There sat the two henny-pennies that had nibbled the doughnut. They didn't seem to be hurt, but their flying leaves lay beside them, crushed up as if the goblins had danced on them with their rat shoes. Polly picked the leaf men up, and Danny and John went off with Ahab toward a big, lonesome sycamore tree in order to find fresh leaves.

"Careful!" Aunty Flo called to them, and John put his hand in his pocket where the glasses were. They would trust to Ahab to sniff out goblins. By then, though, even the goblin laughter had quieted. The fog had drifted away, and the woods were silent and shadowy. They walked around a bend in the trail, and the others were lost to sight behind them.

When they were alone among the quiet trees, the woods seemed almost haunted. John didn't at all want to be there, but there they were. Ahab stayed close, looking to either side as he walked. John shrugged at Danny, who knew what he meant by the shrug. They had promised to fetch two leaves. They had to do their part to help. The sycamore tree wasn't much farther on, and it was a big tree and there would be big leaves roundabout it on the ground.

They walked around another twist of the trail, and there in front of them sat the stone ring, where they had lost the lens yesterday afternoon. It *was* very much like the fountain in the Plaza back home. There was cracked coloured tile around the inside wall, but the glaze was so worn off the tile that you couldn't say exactly what the colours were. It was filled with water that looked muddy, but now, with the sun shining straight through a hole in the trees overhead, they could see that the mud lay on the bottom of the pool and that the water above it was clear. A branch from the big tree threw its reflection across the still water.

"That's the same tree," said Danny suddenly.

"What is?" asked John. "The same as what?"

93

"That big sycamore. It's *our* sycamore. It's the one in the plaza back home, right next to where they put the snowman at Christmas."

John looked hard at the tree, but it didn't take a hard look to see that Danny was right. It *was* the big tree in the Plaza, the compass tree, with its trunk nearly as big around as a wading pool and with four great branches far above the ground, pointing north, south, east, and west.

The wind blew softly out of the east, ruffling their hair. From the tree overhead a lone leaf came drifting and settled on the water. It sailed there like a boat, and its reflection sailed below it.

And then suddenly the leaf was gone, as if it had vanished below the surface of the water. No, not vanished —its reflection was still there. Only it was drifting downward. But because of the sky and the tree reflected on the water, the leaf didn't look as if it were sinking. It looked as if it were rising into the sky of a reflected land.

Then a face peered out of the water at them.

John caught Danny's arm and hopped backward, nearly tripping over Ahab, who was sitting on the ground close behind them. Cautiously, the boys edged forward and looked into the water again. Had it been a goblin?

The face was still there, the face of someone standing in the cloudy-sky world beyond the fountain. It was the little green-hatted man from the curiosity shop. And as John and Danny stood looking at him, he reached up toward them and picked up the reflection of the sycamore leaf.

CHAPTER ELEVEN

THE BEDROOM WINDOW AGAIN

Danny shoved his arm into the water, soaking the sleeve of his jacket. His fingers scraped through the mud at the bottom of the fountain.

"You can't get home that way," said a voice behind them, and both boys jumped when they heard it. Aunty Flo stood there smiling as Danny shook water off his jacket sleeve. "There's enough sun to dry it," she said.

"How *can* we get home?" asked John. "We just saw it, our own town, right here in the water."

"Mr. Deener is the key. He's a very good man, Mr. Deener is."

Danny looked at the muddy sycamore leaf that he had pulled out of the water. He threw it to the ground. It couldn't be the same leaf. "I think he's a very bad man. What's so good about him?"

Aunty Flo looked at her hands for a moment, as if she were studying something, then she said, "He's a good man and he's a bad man. We all are, aren't we? It's a question of what we become—better or worse. Mr. Deener is at war with himself, and you two have come to fight. Just like the henny-pennies, you two are his conscience."

Being someone's conscience seemed hard to John. "How can you be someone else's conscience when your own doesn't always work?" he asked. "I can't tell him anything."

"It works better than you know, this conscience of yours. If it didn't, you wouldn't say that it doesn't always work. If you know that it doesn't always work, then it works pretty well. If you were sure it worked well, then it wouldn't be working very well at all."

John blinked at her, trying to make sense of what she said. It sounded inside out, somehow.

"But what can we tell him?" asked Danny again. "We have to do something. We have to go home. He keeps messing around with doughnuts and jars, but nothing happens except that things get worse."

"You don't have to *tell* him anything. That's part of the problem. He's all his life been telling and telling and telling himself, but he hasn't been listening. He knows that he *should* listen, though, and that makes him mad at himself, and he goes around moaning and groaning and trying to get rid of the feelings that make him so miserable. Right now, it's enough that we help him help you. Then maybe something *will* happen."

She turned away up the path again, and Ahab followed her. John and Danny each picked up a big sycamore leaf off the ground and hurried along after. Polly and Mr. Deener stood right inside the edge of the woods. The leaf men sat on Polly's shoulder and Mr. Deener stood by himself in a sulk.

"They won't speak to me," he said at once to Aunty Flo. "They say this is my fault. But it's just . . . It's just . . . Once they get out of line, they're so hard to get back in."

"Back in where?" Danny asked, showing the henny-pennies the leaf he'd brought with him. One of the little men climbed onto it. A gust of wind took the leaf, and away he sailed into the woods. He looped around once and sailed back out, past Mr. Deener's face, where he floated for a moment, yelling something.

"Back in line," said Mr. Deener to Danny, pretending that the leaf man wasn't there. "Oh bother!" Mr. Deener smashed his eyes shut and covered his ears with his hands. When the little man's companion had climbed onto John's leaf, he flew along after the first, and the two of them were gone out onto the meadow. Mr. Deener sat down among the wildflowers, pointed his soap gun into the air, and shot it. A blast of pink bubbles showered up into the sky and fell onto his head. He sat there thinking, the soap running down his hat and shirt collar.

"He means back inside," said Aunty Flo to Danny.

"Inside where?" asked Danny.

"Can he do that?" John asked. "Can he get the goblins and the henny-pennies back inside him?"

"With help from his friends he might just," she said. Then she walked toward Mr. Deener and said, "The lens, Mr. Deener, Shall we have a go at it?"

"It's no use at all," he told her, not looking up. "We didn't see much. We might just as well eat lunch."

"But remember," said John. "We were going to try to use the spectacles with it."

Mr. Deener stood up tiredly. "I'd forgotten," he said. "That's right. The blasted spectacles." He looked away toward where the henny-pennies had disappeared, and then muttered something that sounded like, "Call me names, will they . . ." Then he said, "Bring them around then. What are we waiting for? Let's have a look. Back to your places with the glass chips then. We've got to set it up all over again." He wiped the soap off his head with the sleeve of his coat.

Aunty Flo and Polly went off across the meadow with their jars, and once again Mr. Deener hunched around, making sure the sunlight swarmed around the meadow in just the right pattern. "It's like music," he said to John. "The melody has to be just right." He motioned Polly over to the left and then adjusted the jar of pond water. Then he waved John over and nodded, as if it were time to pull out the glasses, but somehow he didn't want to come right out and say so.

John reached into his coat for them, but when he handed them across, Mr. Deener leaped back as if they were a poisonous snake. "I don't want them," he said. "Danny, you take them. Now, hold them so . . ." And he made a ring of his thumb and forefinger and held it a foot back from the big isinglass lens. "John, you look through. Won't be any different, I suppose. We're wasting time, is what I think. The sandwiches are drying up, and it looks like the fog's settling in."

Danny held the spectacles just as Mr. Deener had said, and John dropped down onto the ground to look through them. There was no time to think about sandwiches, especially if the fog *was* settling in. Through the spectacles, the meadow was ocean-green, but everything was hazy. "Focus," said John. "Move them back and forth. There! Stop!"

Danny stopped and held very still. The window floated over the meadow again, clear as can be, hanging right above the brushwood. The curtain was open, just as they had left it, and John could see in. There were the bunkbeds against the far wall, and the bookshelf running along above the bed. Their G. Smithers books lay on the shelf. It was all so clear that he could almost read the titles on the books. He scrambled to his feet and took the spectacles so that Danny could look, and then after a moment they switched again.

"Try to touch it!" John said. "I'll keep looking through the lens."

That wouldn't do any good, of course, but they had to try it anyway. Danny went off across the meadow along with Ahab, and John watched, holding the spectacles himself. A curious thing happened.

The window floated away as Danny got nearer. It was exactly like the leaf on the water of the fountain—as if the window were merely the reflection of a window that was drifting away beyond Danny. He never seemed to get any closer to it. The brushwood stayed where it was, but when Danny reached it, the window hung way off over the meadow like a low-flying kite, and Danny poked around in the empty air above the wildflowers and tree branches.

Mr. Deener stood behind John, holding his hat. "Can't quite catch it, then."

John nodded. He couldn't say anything. Seeing the window had made him wonderfully happy, but losing it again almost made it worse than if Mr. Deener's glass magic hadn't worked at all.

"Well," said Mr. Deener. "This is troublesome. Let's try chasing it. We'll put off lunch for another fifteen minutes. We're hungry, but that won't stop us. We'll see if we can't run this window down. Here now! Move in a bit!" He hollered this at Polly and Aunty Flo, who each took five steps in toward the pile of brush.

Mr. Deener hauled the upended picnic baskets, along with their jars of water and tea, a little ways toward the pile of brush. Then he waved Danny back and moved John forward and adjusted the isinglass lens, and there, with the moonlight darting around the meadow again, was the window, closer now to where Danny stood.

They moved it all again, and then again, angling and setting the mirrors—sneaking up on the window, as Mr. Deener put it. He seemed to be full of a growing excitement, and said that he had always wanted to conduct an orchestra, and this was the second best thing, because if he could get all his instruments arranged just so, and all of them playing just the right pattern of notes, why . . .

He didn't say what.

All of them stood in a close circle, now. Overhead, the sun had gotten lost behind the cloud of mist that had come out of the woods, but the moon still showed through it clearly. Moonlight whirled through the glass chips and the jars and the lenses in a little wind devil of light, and John could see the window as if it were two or three feet from him. "It's right there," he said to Danny, but Danny couldn't see anything. He stood on the brush, holding onto Ahab's collar for balance, and waved his hands through the air. Without looking through the lenses himself, though, it was no good. "Just a little bit closer," John said.

"Closer?" asked Mr. Deener. "I'm not sure about closer." He had started to look worried, and was scrunching his face up and squinting, as if he were looking hard at the window himself, as if he could see it now, too, hanging like a ghost over the meadow. He took a step backward.

Aunty Flo nodded at Polly, and both of them reached their jars forward. "Come along, Mr. Deener," Aunty Flo said, sounding like a school teacher. Mr. Deener scrunched up his face even more, as if there was a beehive rather than a window on top of the brush. He bent forward, though, and perched the pondwater and tea and dew and the lump of cheese right at the edge of the basket. He moved the mirrors and the china plates, pushing it all in together so that the whirling moonlight became a little humming ball.

John reached up toward the window. His hand almost brushed the sill. "Closer," he whispered.

But that meant that the jars of glass chips and the isinglass lens must touch the window itself.

And when they did, when the two jars touched the space where the window hung, the moonlight shot straight up into the sky, the big lens broke into bits and fell into the grass, and the window blinked away like a popped soap bubble, and was gone.

"Heck!" John said, standing up.

Then the jar full of pondwater broke, with a thunk, and tumbled off the basket.

"Hey!" cried Mr. Deener.

Then, thunk!—the jar full of morning dew cracked and spilled.

Ahab barked twice and dragged Danny toward the woods.

"My weapon!" shouted Mr. Deener. But when he turned around to go after it, there were six or eight goblins already picking it up out of the grass. Three of them held onto it and a fourth pulled the trigger, spraying pink soap bubbles at Ahab as he danced back and forth barking.

The other two goblins gobbled and laughed, waving and jumping behind their friends. One of them picked up a stone and threw it at John. The other pitched a rock at the jar of green tea, smashing it off the basket.

"Here now!" shouted Mr. Deener, striding toward them. The goblins hunched forward, holding the soap gun like firemen holding a firehose. They turned it on Mr. Deener, showering him with soap. More goblins appeared out of the woods, carrying stones, and began to throw the stones toward the brushwood, trying to break the mirrors and the china plates.

Danny raced back to where John crouched behind the pile of brush. There were plenty of rocks and sticks in the meadow grass. They leaned out from either side and threw rocks just as hard and straight and fast as they could.

100

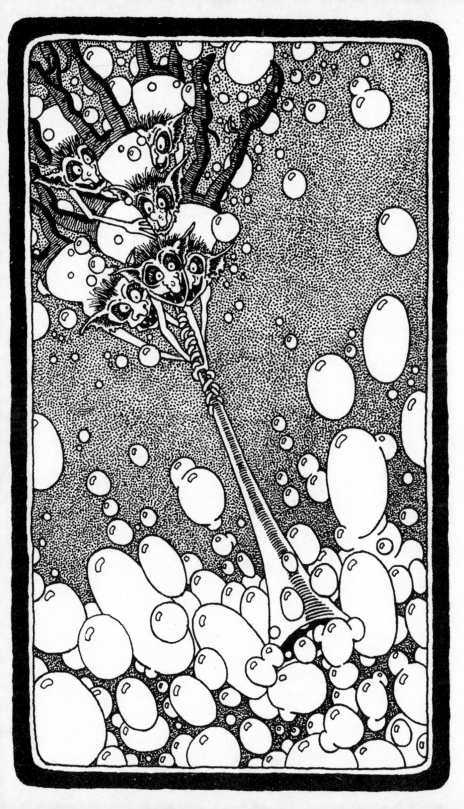

Danny's first rock beaned one of the soap gun goblins on the head, and he dropped the gun and staggered away.

Mr. Deener yelled, as if the rock had hit *him*, and John stood up, took aim, and pounded the closest goblin to him with a rock that hit the little man in the chest. The goblins dropped the soap gun, but wouldn't let Mr. Deener near it. They clustered around in front of it throwing stones. Two more goblins came out of the woods carrying heavy oak sticks about the length of ball bats, and together, keeping behind their companions, they pounded the soap gun to pieces with the sticks.

"By golly" Mr. Deener shouted. And he picked up a rock nearly as big as his head and threw it as hard as he could. It flew about six feet and landed in the weeds. The goblins laughed and laughed and threw handfuls of stones, dancing toward poor Mr. Deener.

John and Danny stepped out from behind the branches, throwing rocks one after another, stopping only long enough to find new ones. Polly and Aunty Flo appeared suddenly at the edge of the woods, behind the goblins. They had sneaked around, carrying the small picnic basket, which they'd filled with river rocks.

The goblins were surrounded. Rocks and sticks rained down on them from front and back. The two that had been smashing the soap gun gave it up, and ran off howling into the trees with Ahab following along behind them. The other goblins threw a few more stones and then broke and ran in two directions. Polly and John and Danny chased them, throwing rocks at their backs, while Mr. Deener danced strangely all alone on the meadow. Each rock that smacked into the back of a goblin seemed to hit Mr. Deener too, and he lurched and jumped there until Aunty Flo shouted for everyone to stop.

John felt a little bit ashamed of himself for having hit goblins in the back with rocks, even after they'd started to run away. But they had broken the big lens. They had wrecked the chance of going home again . . .

Or almost had. The window had blinked away anyway. The mirrors and the bottle glass and all hadn't worked. They needed the spectacles back together again; that was the truth of it. Mr. Deener had been right. They wouldn't get home today, not by messing around out on the meadow, anyway.

Mr. Deener walked across tiredly to the creek, where he washed as much of the soap off himself as he could manage. He didn't even look at his soap gun. It was easy to see, even from a distance, that the gun was a wreck. The goblins had squirted him down and then beat it to bits. "No more stones," he said. "I don't like this stones business."

"Well I like it well enough," said Danny. "I'd like another chance at those goblins. I'd give it to them good." He picked up a stone and threw it at a tree, hitting it with a sharp 'thonk!'

Mr. Deener winced, as if he didn't like the idea of giving it to them good. "Can't we just eat?" he said.

But the lunch was a ruin. When they pulled the sandwiches out of the bottom of the basket they were smashed flat, underneath river rocks. There was mud on what was left of the doughnuts. "Where are the apples?" cried Mr. Deener.

"I think I threw them at the goblins," said Polly. "Sorry."

"Mrs. Barlow!" Mr. Deener shouted. "Mrs. Barlow!" And he stood up and began to hurry along across the meadow, hollering "Mrs. Barlow! Mrs. Barlow! Mrs. Barlow!" as if he were a stuck phonograph record.

By the time that the rest of them had picked up the mirrors and the china plates and the glass jars and the odds and ends of broken stuff and loaded it into the baskets, Mr. Deener was a long way off, trudging up the road toward the house. They could still hear him shouting, and they could see, way off atop the hill, Mrs. Barlow standing among flowerpots on the back patio by the pond, looking down across the railing, watching Mr. Deener heading up the hill toward her.

"We'd better follow along," said Aunty Flo. "If we dawdle now there won't be a scrap of food left in the house. Mr. Deener is in an eating mood."

And with that they set off across the meadow, carrying the baskets and leaving Mr. Deener's broken soap gun lying on the grass.

CHAPTER TWELVE

WHAT BECAME OF THE MOON LADDER

The night was windy and loud. Shrubs and limbs scraped against the laboratory windows, and they could hear the slow creak, creak, creak of bending trees. The moon was high and full, and it shined through the leaves of the trees.

The pieces of moon ladder lay spread out over the floor—the old umbrella and heaped fishing floats, the holly and ivy vines. The rope itself was soft and white and was tied together into a rope ladder with rungs every foot or so. It lay heaped in great straw baskets, the kind you'd imagine a snake living in. There must have been miles and miles of it, because there were dozens of big baskets and every one of them was full of rope ladder.

Mr. Deener stood atop a wooden step stool in the middle of the floor, weaving the last of the holly and ivy into the top of the ladder, which floated in the air like a helium balloon. He explained to John and Danny, who stood below him along with Aunty Flo, that the vine magic would make the top of the ladder climb up the moonlight, just as the vines might climb the wall of a house. What was necessary was that the boys be ready to hang the fishing floats from the ladder every seventeen rungs. They mustn't miss any. This was very delicate, Mr. Deener said from on top of his step stool. Very delicate. The higher the ladder rose into the air, the more it would want to fall, especially with him climbing on it. The glass floats, he said, would give it "bouyancy."

Polly had gone up stairs with Ahab to be with 'the old man,' as Mr. Deener always called him. Neither John nor Danny pointed out that it seemed to be Mr. Deener himself who lay in bed up in the tower. There was no point in saying so, not to Mr. Deener. He would already know it, and, clearly, he didn't at all want to talk about it. Why Polly had to sit with him, John didn't know. Even Mr. Deener didn't seem to be sure. He said simply that he wanted "the poor old man to be safe during the experiment."

The ceiling of the laboratory was high—it must have reached up through the whole house. It looked very much higher than it was, too, because it was dim up there, with only a single little circle of light way off in the shadows, like the moon in a misty evening sky. Light from the lamps burning below seemed to hover around the floor, so that even Mr. Deener's head, a few feet higher than usual because of the step stool, was almost lost in shadow.

"Well," he said to everyone as he climbed down, "are we ready?" He draped the viney end of the ladder over the step stool, tying it there so it wouldn't float away.

"We're ready, Mr. Deener," said Aunty Flo. "Please don't hurt yourself. We need you, you know."

"Nobody needs an old thing like me," he said. "But I don't plan to hurt myself. I've told you, although I don't at all think you believe me or understand, that I'm going home by way of the moon. I intend to come back after you all. I won't abandon you. That's not my way now, nor ever was." He looked very fierce when he said this last, as if maybe he thought someone would suggest otherwise.

"Of course it isn't, Mr. Deener. I'm only asking you to be careful, and not give yourself a knock on the head."

He nodded. "Is Miss Polly with you-know-who, then?"

"Yes," said Aunty Flo, "she is."

"Then," said Mr. Deener excitedly, "there's no time like the president. Hurry up, I've got to catch a bus." He winked at John and Danny and then laughed out loud. "Pack your bags," he said.

Right then he seemed to forget what he was laughing about, and he stood blinking, looking pale and confused. Then he began to haul yards and yards of rope ladder out of

104

the first of the baskets. Aunty Flo looked a little worried.

"Take up that next basket, won't you?" he asked John. "Keep the ladder running out smoothly." He counted down seventeen rungs from the top end and hung two glass floats from it, dangling them from either side in little nets made of string that had been spliced into the rope. "Never two of the same colour together, boys," he said, choosing a blue and a green float.

"That's it—two more floats along down the ladder a ways. It's a cinch. Look for the float nets. Fill them all. Red glass is particularly good for moon travel, but there aren't many red floats, so save them a bit. Portion them out. They're made with melted gold, believe it or not. There! There it goes!"

And just when he said this last sentence, he loosened the ladder where it was tied to the stool. Its vine-hung top began to rise into the air, very slowly, toward the ceiling. With a shout, Mr. Deener hauled the wooden step stool away and then came rushing back and grabbed onto the rope ladder, giving it a pull, as if he wanted to be sure that the whole thing wouldn't come tumbling down. It didn't. It sailed upward toward the circle of light in the ceiling.

It was clearer up toward the ceiling now, as if the light up there had gotten stronger. John and Danny squinted toward it and saw that it wasn't a mere light at all, but that the ceiling itself was set with a window, a great circle of glass, and that moonlight was shining through it. Mr. Deener climbed the ladder, which uncoiled under him, moving upward quicker than he could climb, so that even though he climbed steadily, the ladder went out ahead of him. The end of it, wound with holly and ivy, was quickly lost to sight above.

"The umbrella," said Aunty Flo, picking up the rusty old thing. "What's it for, Mr. Deener?"

"In case it rains!" shouted Mr. Deener, and then he laughed and laughed and rose toward the ceiling. He was happy again, because his ladder was working. Suddenly he stopped laughing, though, and shouted, "The floats!"

John and Danny hadn't been doing their job. They had been watching Mr. Deener and his moon ladder climb away toward the ceiling. They snatched up two floats now, a green and a violet, and hung them in the nets that drifted upward. Then they picked up two more, so as to be ready, and Aunty Flo picked up a couple herself, so as to help. It all went very smoothly—Mr. Deener climbing and climbing, John and Danny sliding glass floats into the nets, the moonlight shining down, brighter now, through the ceiling.

Strangely, after a time it began to look as if Mr. Deener were a mile in the air. And he must nearly have been, too, for the boys had used up sixty or eighty fishing floats. Still the rope ladder slid out of its baskets and up toward the ceiling, and Mr. Deener climbed higher.

Where *was* the ceiling? When the boys looked up, there was Mr. Deener, tiny as a bug, and yet the moon seemed to shine ten thousand miles above him, as if he chased the moon just as Danny had chased the window on the meadow. And there seemed to be no ceiling at all, just the impossibly high walls of the laboratory and the distant sky.

Then there was a shout from above them—not from Mr. Deener, but from Polly. Aunty Flo turned toward the door, hurrying.

"Goblins!" said Danny, although it could only have been a guess. He and John started for the door too, but the ladder kept hauling itself out of the baskets, and two of the string nets slid away into the air without floats in them.

"Darn!" John shouted, turning around to see to the floats. It was too late, though. There they went, far out of reach. "Go!" he said to Danny, and Danny was gone, out the door and up the stairs, following Aunty Flo.

The ladder was slowing down. John could see that. It needed the floats. What would it do? Fall? He couldn't have that. Mr. Deener would come crashing down, and it would be John's fault. He grabbed up two of the floats and started to climb the ladder himself. Maybe he could catch up to the empty nets.

He tucked one of the floats under his chin so as to have his right hand free. There were the nets, right above him. The ladder was barely moving now. Two more nets were just then lifting off the floor, so somehow he would have to hurry down, pick up two more floats, and get them into the nets before those rose into the air too.

The rope ladder stopped. Very softly, from a great distance, Mr Deener shouted a question. John looked up, and there was Mr. Deener, way above him, just a dark speck against the pale white moon, like a flea on a lamp. He couldn't make out what Mr. Deener said, but he could guess. There was no use yelling back. He slid the floats into the nets, and straightaway the ladder began to rise again.

John scrambled toward the floor as quick as he could, but the rope ladder was wiggly beneath him, swaying this way and that way as he shifted his weight climbing down. And it was rising into the air again, quick enough so that he couldn't seem to climb down fast enough. The next pair of empty nets reached him, and again the ladder stopped.

He hurried down now, picked up two floats, and started back up. Then he had an idea: he would slip the floats into the ladder farther down, into what was still piled in the basket. Then he would climb up and fill the two that hovered in the air. That way he could catch up instead of falling further behind. He slid the floats into the closest nets, and then pulled twenty feet of ladder out of its basket and filled the next four nets, laying the ladder back into the basket afterward. Then he picked up a red and a blue float, shoved the red one under his chin, and started up the ladder.

John reached the two empty nets easily, sliding the blue float into one and the red into the other. Everything was going well.

And just then the window slammed open with a bang, and wind gusted through it. The ladder beneath him blew upward in the sudden wind and the room swirled with flying leaves. The ladder in the basket began to rise. It didn't follow the rest of the ladder, either, because the wind blew it back toward the door as its floats tried to rise straight into the air. The ladder looked suddenly more like a rope bridge than a ladder.

Within seconds, forty feet of it hovered in the air like a big W, all of it moving now toward the ceiling. John started climbing and crawling, down and across it, scared of the

107

wind and of the misbehaving ladder. Leaves blew into his face, and he heard, near the window, the sudden laughter of goblins.

The ground looked fearfully far down. His foot slipped through the rungs and he jerked downward, tangled in the rope. He clutched at it, hanging on. Goblins danced on the floor beneath him, laughing and pointing and pretending that they were hanging from a rope ladder too. One of them leaped up to grab the bottom-most part of the ladder, and two of the others, howling and gobbling, gave him a push, so that he swung there, back and forth.

John could hear Mr. Deener's tiny voice shouting above him, and when he looked up, he could see that the whole ladder was swaying back and forth and round and round, like the mast of a ship on a stormy sea.

There was the sudden sound of breaking glass, and John looked down to see one of the goblins smashing a glass float. The others seemed to think it was great fun, and in an instant they were pitching float after float against the wall. Their thin hair flew around their heads in the wind. They looked wild, and there was the awful smell of old fish in the room.

The goblin hanging from the ladder climbed hand over hand until he could yank one of the floats out of its net. He threw it like a baseball, exploding it against the wall. The ladder lurched sideways, but he held on, and pulled out the second float. Straightaway he fell to the ground, onto the heads of his companions, and all of them went down in a gobbling heap, with twenty feet of loose ladder falling on top of them.

They yanked and wiggled and pulled and yelled, and the ladder began to dance and jerk. John held on. Mr. Deener shouted from a hundred miles above them. The moon loomed overhead, big and bright white now, as if John were in the bottom of a deep well and the moon were settling over it like a lid. The two fishing floats below John banged together, and both of them burst. All six of the goblins began to haul themselves up the ladder, scrambling like monkeys.

John pulled himself up, climbing hand over hand, trying

to get away from the goblins. But the farther he climbed from the floor, the scarier it was to climb, and when the goblins got to the next pair of fishing floats, and broke those too, the ladder jerked downward suddenly, and threw John off.

He made a wild grab for the rope and caught himslf halfway to the floor. Almost at once it slipped through his hands, and he felt himself falling again. The crowd of goblins flew past as he rushed downward. He slammed into a half-full basket of rope, smashing the straw sides of the basket and rolling off onto the floor in a tangle of rope ladder.

He sat up, breathing hard. He wasn't hurt, but the fall had scared him silly, and it took a moment for him to think. The goblins scampered farther up the ladder, which was falling as soft and slow as a feather. Rope ladder heaped up on the floor.

John heard the breaking of glass above him and rolled across toward the door in order to get out of the way. The goblins howled with laughter, wrestling with each other and holding on with their legs. The rope ladder seemed to be sliding more quickly toward the ground now.

"Stop!" John yelled, and the goblins yelled, "Stop! Stop! Stop!" and then smashed the next floats. The ladder piled up on the floor, faster and faster, higher and higher. The goblins crashed down howling. Rope ladder fell atop their heads. And way in the air, where the moon filled the entire open ceiling now, Mr. Deener came falling, down and down and down.

CHAPTER THIRTEEN

THE OLD MAN FLOATS AWAY, NEARLY

When Aunty Flo and Danny rushed back downstairs, they found Mr. Deener lying on top of a mountain of cloth rope. John stood beside him, looking at the broken glass, which was everywhere, most of it smashed into little bitty chips. Many of the glass balls weren't broken, but hundreds of them had been, either by the goblins or in Mr. Deener's fall. He lay there on his back like an upside down toad, groaning and looking at the ceiling. The window had been swung open and leaves blew through it, so Aunty Flo scrunched across the glassy floor to shut and latch it. "Goblins?" she asked.

John nodded. "I think he's all right, though. He fell from way up in the sky. There's broken glass everywhere, but he doesn't seem to be cut or anything. Maybe the glass magic protected him."

"No doubt," said Aunty Flo. "Was he a long way up?"

"Nearly to the moon," John said.

"I saw her," mumbled Mr. Deener, as if he were half asleep. "I was almost home."

Aunty Flo gave the boys a look.

"Saw who?" Danny asked.

Aunty Flo said, "His wife, I should think, poor woman. She's been dead these ten years."

"Where did he see her then? On the moon?" Danny looked at John, as if he were thinking that maybe John would know.

"I saw someone too," said John. "It was just before he fell. The moon filled the whole ceiling, and there were the shapes of things on it, sort of like movies on a screen. It was so far away, though, that I can't be sure . . . It was a woman in a kitchen, cooking maybe."

Mr. Deener sat up and looked at the ceiling, which wasn't so very far away at all any more. There was the moon, shining full and high, or maybe it was a lamp way up there. You couldn't really tell anymore. Mr. Deener had a far-off look in his eye as he stared at the distant light. "It was Mrs. Deener. I saw her. She was cooking up something nice for me. I was so *close*. Ten more rungs, and . . ."

"What's wrong, John?" asked Aunty Flo.

"It was *our* kitchen."

"What?" asked Danny. "What does that mean, 'our kitchen'?"

"I'm sure it was our kitchen, at home. I thought it was mom cooking. But it wasn't her. It was somebody a little fatter, and in an old sort of apron. But it *was* our kitchen."

"Who was it?" asked Danny.

"It was Mrs. Deener," said Aunty Flo.

"I wasn't ten steps away," said Mr. Deener, and he stared away through the window for a moment before shutting his eyes and falling asleep.

"At our house?" Danny whispered.

This didn't make a lick of sense to John either, but he was determined suddenly that it should. "Why was our kitchen on the moon," he asked, "and what was Mrs. Deener doing in it? Was she *really* in it, or was that some sort of trick?"

"It hasn't always been your kitchen, has it?"

Both boys shook their heads. Of course it hadn't been. The house was sixty years old.

"It was Mr. Deener's house too?" Danny asked.

"And a very jolly house it was," said Aunty Flo. "Until she died. That's why he sold it. He couldn't stand being there without her. They had been together in that house for nearly forty years. He saw her everywhere in it, even after she had died. She had sewn the curtains and cooked the food and bought the carpets. She had sat a thousand times

112

in all the chairs, and every night they had slept in the same bed. There she was, wherever he looked."

Aunty Flo stopped for a moment, as if she were making sure that she was telling the story right. "Of course it wasn't *really* her, left over in the house after she died, any more than it was really her in the moon kitchen just now. It was just reflections of her, memories of her, and that's what he couldn't stand. He sat in the empty house all day and thought about her until he began to forget how to think about anything else."

"What did he do?" asked John, who knew how bad it was to sit and think about troublesome things.

Danny shook his head. "Why didn't he just *quit* thinking about it. Why didn't he *do* something? Go fishing or something?"

"He tried to," Aunty Flo said. "He moved away and lived alone and dabbled with his glass magic, trying to build a sort of lens that would let him see her as she had been—really see her. And he did build it, too, but it made him even sadder to see her and still not be with her. And still, what he saw was the reflection of her in his memory. But he thought now that if she could live in the land of memory, then he would learn to travel there too."

This was confusing, all this 'land of memory' business. It sounded to John as if it would be a troublesome place.

Aunty Flo went on with her story. "So one sort of magic led to another. He tried very hard, but he couldn't enter where she lived, and the sorrow of it drove him finally to break himself in half, to put the sad half of himself to sleep, in order to forget. I think, though, that the sleeping half of him searches for her in his dreams. Anyway, it was then that he came to live here. Half of him is intolerably sad, and he sleeps all the time in the tower upstairs, and when he awakens, he can't see what you and I see. As I said before, he isn't blind. But in the past he had made himself see too much, and so now he doesn't let himself see at all. He can't let her go, and he can't go home again either."

"Can *we* go home again?" asked John. Suddenly he was certain that all this glass magic had worked to make things worse for Mr. Deener rather than better, and this meant, maybe, that it would make things worse for him and Danny, too.

"Of course you can. It's still your home. Everything you love is there, waiting for you. But you can't go home by way of the moon or by any other imaginary path. You've got to go straight back in through the window. And you've got to take Mr. Deener with you."

"But . . ." Danny started to say. John knew what he was thinking. It wasn't at all clear how they would do this. "Can he help us?"

"I think," said Aunty Flo, "that you'll help each other, and all get home by dinnertime. Polly and I will help too, and Mrs. Barlow. She's really very fond of Mr. Deener, you know. She seems hard on him, but what she wants is to put him back together again, and she has to work at it in her own way."

John and Danny started talking at once. There was so much to know, so much to understand. How were they to help Mr. Deener? How were they to repair the spectacles?

Mr. Deener himself was asleep way up on top of his heap of rope. It couldn't have been a very nice bed, but he seemed to be woefully tired, so it didn't matter.

"It's late," said Aunty Flo. "No more questions tonight. There's nothing more to be done. In the morning I'll show you a little something."

Polly and Ahab arrived just then from upstairs. "He's sleeping nicely now," Polly said to Aunty Flo, nodding toward the door. There was a tapping on the window just then, like someone knocking with the stems of leaves. Polly opened the window and a scattering of sycamore leaves blew into the room. Henny-penny men rode on the leaves, having a look around. Two of them landed on Mr. Deener's shoulder and began straightaway to whisper into his ear. He mumbled something and half smiled, and the little men whispered some more. Polly closed the window.

The rest of the henny-pennies landed and then dragged their leaves off into a corner. They rolled up their sleeves and started picking up pieces of glass, laying the pieces in piles according to colour. Aunty Flo and Polly and John and Danny tiptoed out the door and went upstairs to bed,

114

leaving the henny-pennies to clean up the laboratory while Mr. Deener slept on his mountain of rope.

The bedroom was dark except for candlelight, and the house was quiet. A draft blew in under the windows and made the candle flame dance, so that little shadows leaped and fell on the wall behind the beds. John wasn't sleepy at all. Too much had happened that night, and he had only seen part of it. He had to know what had gone on upstairs, with the Old Man. It was beginning to seem as if Mr. Deener was a complete failure. He was very sure of himself, and he could do some very clever tricks with pieces of glass, but all of his clever tricks turned into junk, finally. Why couldn't he see that? Was it because he didn't *want* to see it?

It was clear, from what Aunty Flo said, that they would get home only with Mr. Deener's help. But there he lay, right now, on top of his rope pile, everything having gone to smash around him. It seemed as if every time he started to work his magic, the goblins danced in and broke it all up. At this rate they would never get home.

They had to do something for Mr. Deener, to help him help himself, so that then he could help them. But what? What could they do? He didn't seem to want or need their help, except for the business of loading fishing floats into the nets. But that was a wreck now, and it was largely John's fault. Or at least that's what he thought as he lay there in the candle-lit darkness, listening to the wind.

He didn't like the idea of it being his fault. He didn't like the whole idea of faults. Clouds passed across the moon outside, and suddenly moonlight streamed through the window, onto the bed covers. John got the spectacles out of his jacket and held them up so that the moonlight shined through the green lens and into his face. It didn't do any good.

What had he expected? Half of him wished that he could work Mr. Deener's glass magic, that he could turn a little part of his worries into a goblin. He would throw it out the window into the pond, and then he would never again

115

worry that something had been his fault. But the idea of there being a bunch of smelly old goblins out in the night, all of them looking like him, was even worse than his worrying, and he put the spectacles away. They hadn't done anything but cause trouble anyway. And there wasn't any magic in them now that they were broken.

"So what happened upstairs?" John asked Danny, who had been quiet for the past five minutes.

"What?" Danny asked, almost asleep. He leaned on his hand and elbow. "It was weird," he said, yawning. "The old man nearly floated away."

"Floated away?"

"That's right. That's why Polly yelled. He was floating on the ceiling, bumping it with his nose. When we got up there he was almost over the stairs, so that if he fell, it might have killed him."

"Wow," said John. "How come?"

"How come what?"

"How come he was floating?"

"Who knows? He was like a balloon. We had to tie a string to him and pull him back in, over the bed."

"How did you do that? Climb up onto a chair?"

"We tried that, but he was too high. The ceiling is way up there. So I climbed up onto that big cabinet against the wall and tied the belt from his bathrobe around his foot. Aunty Flo pulled him back into the room. He didn't want to come down, though."

"What do you mean, he didn't *want* to?"

"You know, he kept floating back up. We would have had to sit on him or something or tie him to the bed."

John nodded and watched the flickering candle flame. "I think I know why he was floating," he said.

"Why?"

"He was going with Mr. Deener, to the moon. He really is Mr. Deener, and Mr. Deener can't get away without taking the Old Man along. That's what I think. I bet he fell onto the bed when Mr. Deener fell downstairs."

"Not onto the bed. Goblins crawled in through the window and were running around, causing trouble. Aunty Flo was chasing them when there was all the shouting and

breaking from downstairs, from down where you were. Then the Old Man fell onto the goblins. He nearly squashed one of them. He just went to sleep there on the floor."

"The goblin did?"

"No, the Old Man. Me and Polly lifted him back onto the bed. He didn't weigh hardly anything. It was like he was made out of air or something."

"What did Polly say?"

Danny looked at him and then smiled. "What do you mean, 'what did Polly say'? Why do you want to know? Don't worry about it."

"I'm not worrying. What do you mean, 'don't *worry* about it'? Who's worrying?"

"You are."

"Am not."

"Are too."

John lay there for a while, not saying anything. Finally he said, "Anyway, what I think is that . . ." but he realized that Danny had fallen asleep again. It was no use talking to him, and besides, he didn't have much new to say anyway. He lay there thinking about things, about Mr. Deener and about Aunty Flo, about his parents and what was going on back home. Were they asleep? Were they worrying about him? He began to worry about them worrying, but then he made himself stop worrying and start thinking about Polly instead, and how much she looked like Kimberly. Things were happening to him, and to Danny too, but he didn't know what they were. He was caught up in a mystery that was as strange as any dream he had ever had.

When he fell asleep, though, he didn't wish that he would wake up at home and that everything would be all right. Wishing and hoping wasn't going to work. That was Mr. Deener's mistake. They had to *do* something, but he had no idea what.

CHAPTER FOURTEEN

WHAT THEY SAW IN THE FOUNTAIN

John and Danny got up early. Aunty Flo had said that she would show them something, and they were ready to see it, whatever it was.

The laboratory was swept clean. The rope ladder had been heaped back into the baskets, and the baskets set against the wall. The glass chips must have been poured into jars. Every last one was gone from the floor. Aunty Flo slipped in and took a jar from a shelf. It was filled with chips of a dozen colours, all mixed up together like Christmas candy.

Mrs. Barlow made them a breakfast of scrambled egg sandwiches on toast, which wasn't just what they wanted. But they were hungry, and they ate the sandwiches on the road to the meadow. Mrs. Barlow had been happy and whistling merrily. Aunty Flo said it was because Mr. Deener hadn't been able to go home by way of his moon ladder. Mrs. Barlow, she said, saw a better way to take him home. Food magic—that was the way of Mrs. Barlow. John hoped she was right.

On the way down the hill, Polly fed part of her egg sandwich to Ahab, who seemed to like it pretty well, and John told her about how he and Danny sometimes had breakfast at Watson's. He told her about the pancakes and sausages and hot chocolate and about how he and Danny would ride down there on Saturday mornings together. Polly said she wished she could go along, just the three of

119

them, and then said that Mrs. Barlow made maybe the best pancakes in the world. Then John said that he wished they all lived in the same world, and for a couple of minutes Polly didn't say anything at all.

It was a pretty morning, sunny and already warming up, with just a hint of a cool breeze. Away above them lay the sleeping land, with its brown trees and grass and muddy river. The dry grass seemed to have edged closer to the house on the hill, creeping up on it.

Soon they were on the meadow and walking toward the path that lead to the fountain. There everything was green and growing. John could feel how lonesome it was, though, and ever since Polly had grown quiet, it seemed that there was some of the loneliness in her, too. There was the feeling in the air that, even out here on the meadow, the wildflowers and meadow grasses would soon begin to fall asleep too, as if the whole land belonged in some way to Mr. Deener. As if the land *was* Mr. Deener.

"Remember that it's still only *part* of the land that's asleep," said Aunty Flo suddenly, turning her head and saying it loud enough so that John could hear.

"Will it wake up?" asked Danny, "Or will the rest of it fall asleep?"

Aunty Flo shrugged. "We'll yell in its ear," she said.

"Do you have a bicycle?" John asked Polly.

She shook her head. "There's nowhere to ride one, I guess. Not around here."

"Are there any other kids around?"

"Just you and Danny," she said.

"That's all? Ever? Who do you play with?"

"The leaf men, mostly. I sew clothes for them and they bring me things. Treasures, you know. Pretty things they've taken away from the goblins. They love to play cards and hide and seek and all."

"Cards? The little men?"

"It's because Mr. Deener loves to play cards, or used to. He doesn't do much any more except magic."

In the morning sunlight, Polly reminded John of Kimberly again. But when he tried to see Kimberly's face in his mind, what he saw was Polly's face instead. The same was true of

120

Aunty Flo. She looked just like Mrs. Owlswick—more so all the time. Or did Mrs. Owlswick look like her? Maybe that was the same thing. He tried to imagine Mrs. Owlswick's face, but he couldn't. All he could see was Aunty Flo, as if there had never been a Mrs. Owlswick.

The idea scared him. He wondered what it meant. Was he forgetting things about his neighbourhood, about where he lived? Had his memory started to get lost when he and Danny had got lost? He thought hard for a moment, biting his lip. He hadn't forgotten Harvey Chickel's face. He could see that easily. And Mrs. Webostad, his teacher at school—he could see her too. And his mother and father and Shirley next door and Joseph, one of his best friends. All of them were right there in his mind, clear and close. So he wasn't forgetting. He didn't have to worry. He hadn't lost anything at all.

He quit biting his lip and said, "Have you always lived here?"

"What do you mean?" asked Polly. "I guess so."

"Did you come from somewhere? I mean, are there, like, cities or something around here?"

She shrugged, almost as if she didn't know what he was talking about. "We stay pretty much around home. Mr. Deener can't be left alone for too long. He's always up to some kind of magic, like his moon ladder. You never know what he'll do with it. One time he made the whole house disappear. We were working in the vegetable garden and it was just gone. Just like that. Aunty Flo had to get it back again. And once he made it rain marbles. Just for a moment, to see if he could do it. Mrs. Barlow was out on the lawn and got hit in the head, and she wouldn't make him doughnuts for two days after that until he promised to be good."

"But *are* there towns and like that? Back up in the hills maybe?"

"I guess so," Polly said. "They'd mostly be asleep, though. Sometimes I see lights at night, from my window. And once I saw something flying. I guess it was an airplane. But it was so far away that it might have been a bird or something that Mr. Deener had dreamed up."

"Where was the airplane going?"

"I don't know. Where do they go?"

"Places," said John. "They go to places." This kind of talk was starting to scare him again. "How do you know about airplanes if you never see them?"

"I remember them," she said. "And there's pictures in books. And anyway, it was probably something Mr. Deener dreamed up, like I said. Do you remember when you first saw an airplane?"

John shook his head. He didn't, really. He couldn't remember when he first had seen anything. Some things had always been there, hadn't they? Just like old Ahab. There had never been a time when Ahab hadn't been around. And he couldn't remember not having been able to walk or talk or drink a glass of milk. He had been a baby once, but he couldn't remember when. He wished that he *could* remember when he had first seen an airplane—what it looked like, how it sounded. But he couldn't. So why should Polly?

But the idea of Polly and Aunty Flo always having been living there, digging in their garden and walking on the meadow and taking care of Mr. Deener—there was something about it that John didn't understand. "What about Mrs. Barlow?" he asked. "Where is she from?"

Polly shrugged. "She came years ago. She knew Mr. Deener from a long time ago, and came to help one day. She just came to the door. I don't know how she got here. Same way as you, maybe."

"Through our bedroom window?"

"You didn't just come through your bedroom window, either, you know. You had to be helped through it."

It seemed to John as if all of this was true, and yet none of it explained anything at all. Suddenly he was full of questions, about Mr. Deener and Polly and Mrs. Barlow and what kind of magical land it was where Mr. Deener could make it rain marbles and where maybe there were towns back up the valley and maybe there weren't. But before he could ask any of those questions, Polly started running to catch up with Danny and Aunty Flo, who were just then going into the woods. John ran after her, not wanting to be by himself.

In minutes they stood in front of the fountain in the middle of the quiet trees. The water was dark and still. John imagined that he was home in Orange, standing in the Plaza. Behind him would be the Continental Cafe, and across from him would be the curiosity shop and the beauty college. Off to the right was Watson's drug store with its pancakes and milk shakes. He wished he were really there.

Aunty Flo took out the jar full of glass chips and poured them slowly into the water, around and around so that they sank in a circle the size of a bicycle tire. They fell to the bottom, blue and red and green and yellow, glinting in the sunlight that shone through the big sycamore behind them. The bits of glass disappeared, though, when they got to the muddy floor of the fountain.

Then, just as the last of them settled into the darkness, it seemed as if someone had switched on a light beneath the water. It was a pale rainbow, swirling around and around, the colours mixing up together in a milky circle. Then everything was still again, and it seemed for all the world as if the moon were reflected on top of the water.

It *was* the moon, too—as it would look if you saw it through a telescope, with mountains and valleys and dry riverbeds. The Man in the Moon looked up at them out of the reflection. His face was a trick of shadows. It looked awfully familiar, though, that face did—so familiar that Danny asked, "Who is that?"

"It's Aiken Drum," said Aunty Flo.

"Aching Who?" asked John, but then he remembered the rhyme in the G. Smithers book, and he knew who it was.

The shadows on the moon started to shift and swirl just then, and suddenly it wasn't the moon any more at all. It was something very much like Mr. Deener's big isinglass lens that seemed to be reflected there, atop the waters of the old ruined fountain.

Beneath it, or through it, they could see the Plaza, downtown. There was the fountain, the palm trees and the sycamores. There were the sidewalks that cut the circular plaza into pie pieces. The trees were small, though, as if they had just been planted, and the buildings around the

123

Plaza were different. There was a horse cart jingling around and up the street. They could hear the noise of it, and could hear the horse whinny. Then an old car, like a buggy on wheels, came chug-chugging along Chapman Avenue, driven by a man in a hat. Dust blew up from beneath the tires. What they were looking at was the Plaza a long, long time ago.

Aunty Flo dipped her hand in the water and gave it a bit of a stir. The reflection broke to pieces, but then unbroke itself and came back together as the water calmed. There was the Plaza again, except that the trees were bigger. There were rose bushes now, and the faces of some of the buildings had been changed. There were men in overalls painting. Two kids on bicycles rode across the street, toward Watson's.

"It's you!" Polly said.

And it was. Maybe it was a Saturday morning.

Then in a blink the Plaza was gone. Their house on Pine Street appeared, but without the carport on the side, and with a different front door. It wasn't their house yet. It was the house as it had been when it belonged to someone else, when it was full of someone else's memories. The old porch was the same, though, and it was still half lost in sunny green shadows. Someone stood on it. It was Mr. Deener, looking very young. He had just got home, it seemed. The door opened, and a woman appeared.

"That's her!" said John.

"Who?" asked Danny. "It's no one I've ever seen before."

"Last night—the woman on the moon."

"Mrs. Deener," said Aunty Flo.

Happy laughter sounded on the breeze. They could hear the door click shut.

Then, overhead, a cloud passed over the sun, and the picture in the water got dim and confused. When the sun shined again, there was Mr. Deener, standing once more on the front porch. He held his hat in his hand while he fumbled in his pocket for his key. He seemed to be in an awful hurry. He was bald on top, now, and fatter. Time had gone by, just like that, in an instant. He threw his hat down onto the floor of the porch and worked the key into the

124

lock. He pushed the door open and went in. They could hear his voice calling and calling.

"What's wrong?" asked Danny. "What's happened?"

"She's died," said Aunty Flo, "and Mr. Deener has come home too late."

Neither John nor Danny said anything for a moment. The reflection of the house lingered there on top of the water until Aunty Flo dipped her hand in and swirled it again.

"Could he have done anything about it?" asked John, hoping, of course, that he couldn't have. If he could have, then he would have to worry about it forever. Poor Mr. Deener, he would worry about it anyway. John knew he would.

"There was not a living thing he could do," she said. "But he won't be convinced of it, will he? He won't let himself believe it. He's full of fault and blame. Look."

Their house had disappeared. There was the Plaza again, but now with the fountain dry and full of dead leaves and mud. The grass was brown, and the rose bushes were thorny and overgrown and hadn't a green leaf on them. The trees were dead too. The little redwood tree that they had just last year planted as a Christmas tree was droopy and brown. It looked as if bugs had been at it. Store windows were broken. Everything was grey and asleep, covered in a heavy layer of dust. The fountain was broken, too, and had begun to look very much like the fountain in the woods.

Something moved across the street from the sleeping Plaza. There it was again—behind a brick planter that was cracked half to pieces and filled with dark weeds. It was a goblin. He scampered down the street, stopped before a broken shop window, and climbed through. It wasn't just any shop, either; it was the curiosity shop, deserted now.

A moment later a fish skeleton with the head still on it sailed out through the window and landed on the pavement among a litter of old newspapers and broken bottles. The wind blew down the street, picking up the newspapers and rushing them along. They heard goblin laughter on the wind. And way down the road, just disappearing in the distance, was a little man dressed in green, with what might have been a bundle of sticks on his back. They knew who he was, and they knew he was leaving.

"Show us our house again," said Danny.

Almost as quickly as he said it, there it was. The grass in the front yard was weedy and high and brown, and the bushes around the front porch were dead. Flower pots lay broken and spilling out dusty soil in front of the door. Windows were cracked and broken. Everything was dirty and old, as if it had stopped living, as if time had stopped and only goblins moved through the neighbourhood. One poked his head out of the crawlspace under the house. It didn't look like Mr. Deener; it looked like Harvey Chickel.

"It's Harvey," said John.

"Turned into a goblin," said Danny.

"I don't think I like him," Polly said.

"Some people don't need glass magic to turn themselves into goblins," said Aunty Flo. "They like a broken world better than a world that's whole. They can't stand to be the only broken thing."

John suddenly put his hand in the water and stirred it up. He didn't want to see any more. The house vanished, and there was nothing left when the water calmed but the reflection of the moon again. He and Danny would put a stop to this business of everything going to sleep, of things being broken. Harvey Chickel wasn't a goblin yet. He was cracked, maybe, but he wasn't broken. All of them were cracked in some little way.

Mr. Deener and Harvey Chickel were Humpty Dumpties, but they hadn't fallen so hard that they couldn't be put back together again. Or at any rate, John and Danny would *try* to put them back together again, starting with Mr. Deener. They had to pull out the glue pot and try.

The wind blew up just then, ruffling the surface of the water. Clouds crossed the sky again. The reflection was gone, and the fountain fell into shadowy darkness. They could still hear goblin laughter, but now it came from the deep woods, and they could see that the fog was drifting toward them. Without anyone saying anything they turned to leave.

126

On the meadow they slowed down just a little, and John asked, "Did all that happen?"

"All what?" asked Aunty flo.

"All that we saw."

"Mostly."

"How about that last bit?" asked Danny. "Has it happened too? How long have we really been gone from home? That must have taken years. It couldn't have happened since the day before yesterday."

"You've been gone just the blink of an eye," she said. "No, it hasn't happened yet, not like that. But I'm afraid it all rather depends on Mr. Deener, doesn't it? Part of him, his shadow, let's say, is still living in your world, in your town. There are shadow goblins, too. And of course there are people like your friend who have too many shadows in them. I'm afraid, though, that if Mr. Deener gets worse, and reduces himself to nothing here, then the goblins in your world will be more than mere shadows."

John gave Danny a look, and they told Aunty Flo about the Plaza, about people falling asleep and glass jewelry being stolen and all the rest. Suddenly it wasn't just the problem of the broken spectacles that troubled them, or the notion of their parents worrying. Now it was clear that Mr. Deener's troubles were their own troubles whether they wanted them or not.

That's the way it was, John thought. Like goblins, trouble would find you. You couldn't hide from it or pretend it wasn't there. You couldn't always be slipping out from under it, as Mr. Deener tried to do. You had to do something about it finally.

When they were on their way up the hill, tramping along between the trees, they saw a jar broken on the road, spilling green glass chips into the dirt. Aunty Flo stopped to look at it for a moment, and then all at once hurried along toward home. A hundred yards farther up they found one of Mrs. Barlow's china plates, broken and lying in the weeds.

"Goblins," said Danny.

Aunty Flo shook her head. She looked worried. "I hope so."

That was an odd thing, her saying that. But Polly must

127

have known what Aunty Flo meant, because she was already running up the road toward home. The three of them hurried along after her, and when they got to the house, John and Danny found out what she meant. Mr. Deener was gone.

That was worse than goblins. If he had gone away to lose himself in some last bit of glass magic, then they might never get him back. His moon ladder hadn't worked; it had only made him more sorrowful than ever. Maybe he had gotten tired of making goblins, of breaking himself up a piece at a time. Maybe he had found a way to lose himself forever.

They looked high and low, upstairs and down. They looked in the root cellar and out in the garden. They shouted Mr. Deener's name off the balcony. Upstairs, the sleeping Mr. Deener slept as ever, but it was a troubled sleep, and he seemed to be trying to talk to someone. He mumbled and turned and twisted. His feet stirred beneath the covers, as if he thought he were walking somewhere. In the kitchen they found Mrs. Barlow, mixing up dough for the doughnuts. She hadn't seen Mr. Deener either. He hadn't come in for breakfast.

"Not come in for breakfast!" said Aunty Flo. "He's gone out for sure, then. And he's not himself, either. He's in terrible trouble. We have to find him."

"Where?" asked Mrs. Barlow, wiping her hands on her apron. "There's no place for him to go."

"He's gone off to build his castle, probably. It's very near the end unless we can stop him." Aunty Flo put her hand to her forehead as if she were thinking.

John wasn't happy to hear talk about 'the end.' And from the look on his face, Danny wasn't either.

"We'll find him," Danny said.

"Sure we will," John said, but he wondered just how they would find him. Mr. Deener hadn't gone down onto the meadow. They would have seen him if he did. He had probably gone into the woods, into the fog and the shadows.

"We'll take old Ahab," said Danny. "He'll sniff Mr. Deener out."

128

"If only these doughnuts were ready," Mrs. Barlow said. "They'd fetch him home."

"But they aren't ready," said Aunty Flo. "And with every minute that passes, Mr. Deener slips farther and farther away. You two had better go, doughnuts or no doughnuts. Mrs. Barlow and Polly can follow along. Whatever he's up to, try to stop him. Try to hold him up until help comes."

"Tell him there's doughnuts coming," Mrs. Barlow said. "Six dozen glazed. He can eat the whole lot of them."

"I'll go with John and Danny," Polly said, pulling on her sweater."

"Wait for Mrs. Barlow," Aunty Flo said, winking at her. "She can't be expected to travel in the woods alone. The boys will make their own way this time."

"Take these cookies, then," said Mrs. Barlow, handing them a little bag. "And save them for the Deener. They'll keep him occupied till the doughnuts come. Hurry!"

Danny slipped the cookies into his backpack and put it on over his jacket.

"So we're going alone?" asked John.

"There's three of you," said Aunty Flo. "Ahab will go along. You're not alone at all. There's nothing in the woods but trees. Here, take these, though, just in case. A good stick is usually enough to scare the goblins off."

John wondered what she meant by using the word 'usually.' What if the goblins wouldn't be scared off?

She stepped across to a stand near the door and pulled out two walking sticks. They were straight canes cut out of oak—just the right sort of thing to bonk goblins with. The two of them took the sticks, and Danny held his in two hands like a baseball bat, and swung it at an imaginary goblin. But John knew, as they went out through the front door and down the hill, that carrying a stick in your hand didn't make the woods any less dark. And sticks wouldn't make Mr. Deener come home, either. That would take a different sort of knock on the head.

CHAPTER FIFTEEN

IN THE DEEP WOODS

Tracking Mr. Deener was easy. Ahab hurried along in front of them, sniffing the ground. Partway down the hill he found the broken plate, and he stood next to it wagging his tail. John and Danny patted him and told him it was a wonderful thing, finding a broken plate like that. Looking happy, he trotted along farther, looking this way and that way. He stopped once to chase a lizard and another time to chase a bug. When he found the broken jar, though, he barked twice and danced around it, looking back up toward where John and Danny were coming along down the road.

"Good boy!" said Danny when they caught up.

"Find something more!" said John, hoping that there was something more to find. Mr. Deener must have gone into the woods with more stuff than he could carry.

Ahab sniffed along for a way and then pushed straight in among the bushes and trees. John and Danny ran to where he had disappeared. A little trail cut through the brush, just wide enough for them to go along Indian file. Ahab stood ahead, looking down at a pocket handkerchief.

"Mr. Deener's handkerchief," said Danny.

John looked at it. "How do we know?"

"Ahab says it is. That's why he found it. He's sniffing out Mr. Deener, just like a bloodhound. Good boy," Danny said, patting Ahab on the head again. "We should have brought some treats for him."

"We should have brought some treats for us," John said.

"I guess you're right, though. Whose handkerchief would it be if it weren't Mr. Deener's?"

Maybe a goblin's, John thought, but he didn't say so. Besides, why would goblins carry handkerchiefs? They didn't have any manners at all. They'd blow their noses on their bat shirts.

Ahab was off again, very serious now. They followed him deeper into the woods, where it was shadowy and dark in among the great oak trees. Here and there a little bit of sunlight shined through the leaves, like scattered gold on the forest floor.

They found a sprinkling of glass chips from a leaking jar. And once, when they'd gone about half a mile and hadn't found any clues at all, three sycamore leaves sailed past with henny-penny men sitting on them. One of the leaves made a turn around John's head, and he heard the little man yell something before he whizzed away, but he couldn't make out what it was.

They were on Mr. Deener's trail, right enough. They hurried along now, nearly running, holding their sticks like spears. Ahab bounded ahead, barking now and again when he found more glass chips. It seemed to be growing darker, although it couldn't be past eleven in the morning. The sun didn't shine through the leaves and limbs overhead any more. It was as if they were walking through a great cave under a mountain. It had gotten cooler, too, and wetter.

"Fog," Danny said. He stopped and pointed up into the trees. There was a sort of clearing above them, and they could see the grey and misty sky easily now. They stood in silence, listening. Way off in the distance they could hear the sound of waves breaking. They must have got very close to the sea. The bushes were thicker roundabout them, and the trees were hung with vines and moss. John zipped his jacket up, and both boys put up their hoods.

It was then that they saw the fire through the trees. It seemed to be a campfire, burning in the darkness of the deep woods. Ahab saw it too, but instead of running toward it to investigate, he sat down on the path, cocked his head, and watched it.

"Mr. Deener," said John.

"I guess so," Danny replied. "Maybe."

"Who else?"

Danny shrugged.

John thought about it. It might, certainly, be Mr. Deener. There seemed to be another little path or game trail leading off in that direction. If it *was* Mr. Deener, then it was foolish to go on. Going on would be to waste time, and Aunty Flo had said that they hadn't any time to waste. If it wasn't Mr. Deener, then who was it? Goblins?

"Remember that fire that we saw from the tower window," John said.

Danny nodded. "Do you think this is the same fire?" he asked.

"Might be. But then it might be Mr. Deener's fire, too. We don't know. We've got to find out, though."

They could sneak down the trail, keeping low and holding their whacking sticks ready. They would only get close enough to see if it was Mr. Deener. There was no going on without knowing for certain.

Ahab led the way. He didn't seem to want to. Now and then he growled, very softly, and stopped to sniff the misty air. They stooped along, stepping carefully, pushing leafy branches out of their way as well as they could. For a moment they lost sight of the fire beyond a little bend in the trail. There it was again.

They stopped for a moment. The fire seemed farther away now, and seemed to lie in a different direction, off to their right. The fire leaped and then died down and then leaped again, as if someone were throwing handfuls of dry leaves on it. They crept nearer. They hadn't gone far. They could always find their way back to the path.

Shadows rose and fell on the trees beyond the fire. They sneaked along, very close now, but still they could see no one, nothing but dancing shadows. The bushes and vines and trees and creepers were too thick.

Then, suddenly, the fire blinked out. It was gone, just like that. And almost as suddenly it blinked on again, a ways farther into the woods. They edged closer once more, silent and careful.

A flute began to play, very thin and distant. Ahab

growled. John took him by the collar and edged around the trunk of an enormous oak tree, climbing up onto a big tangle of roots so that he might get a better look. But just as he peered around the edge of the tree, the fire was gone again and the woods were dark. Then there it was, burning brightly, way off in the distance.

"I don't like this," said John, holding onto Ahab and looking back over his shoulder. "Something's wrong. That isn't Mr. Deener."

Goblin laughter sounded from somewhere far away, just the hint of it.

"It's a trick," said Danny. "Let's go."

They turned and started back, letting Ahab go along first. The fog had drifted in though, and was thick and grey. There was brush where the trail ought to have been. The pushed through it, but it just got thicker and thicker, so again they turned around and pushed back out. It seemed as if the trail had gotten lost. They tripped over mossy stones and climbed over fallen logs. Ahab sniffed this way and that way. The only sound in the misty air was the laughter of goblins and the hollow piping of flutes that sounded almost like wind chimes.

Then, just when it seemed they were altogether lost, there was the great oak tree again, and the goblin fire burning—far off now, flickering and shifting. They *had* been tricked. There was no path anywhere, just fog and heavy green leaves. They could still hear the sound of breaking waves, but it was hard to tell where it came from. It sounded almost as if it were all around them. Even that might have been goblin trickery.

"Maybe the henny-pennies will save us," John said. But he knew they wouldn't. He was just trying to be hopeful. How would the little men on leaves find them way out in the middle of the forest?

"They won't," said Danny. "I'm going to climb this tree. It's the biggest tree around, and it looks easy enough to climb. If I could get up into the top branches, I might be able to see something—the ocean, the house, anything."

John looked up into the tree. It *was* a good climbing tree. It had about a million heavy limbs, and as was true of old oak

134

trees, most of the leaves grew out at the ends of the limbs.
"*I'll* do it," John said. He didn't want to, but he didn't want
Danny to have to do it either. It was time to be responsible.
He noticed that the fog was thicker, and it was darker than
ever in the woods.

"No, I'll climb it." Danny shook his head. "I'm a better
climber."

John started to argue with him. "I'm not afraid to," he
said.

"Who said you were?"

"Nobody. But I should do it."

"Why?" Danny asked. "I didn't say you were afraid; I said
I was a better climber."

And it was true. Danny *was* a better climber. John
shrugged. It was time for him to stop being afraid of other
people thinking he was afraid. He bent over to help boost
Danny onto the lowest branch. "Be careful," he said. "If
you can see anything, figure out which one of the limbs is
pointing toward it, and we'll set out in that direction, lining
up points in order to go in a straight line."

Danny was already up into the tree, hauling himself
from branch to branch. He was staying in toward the
trunk, where there were knotholes and broken limbs to
hold onto. The silvery-grey bark looked slippery to John,
from where he stood down below, and the fog wouldn't
make things any easier. It was a dangerous thing for Danny
to do, and all at once John started to think that he shouldn't
have let him do it, that they should have tried something
else first. But of course they *had* tried something else first.
John watched, shouting for Danny to be careful. And then,
in an instant, fog blew in, and Danny vanished in it.

John yelled, and Danny yelled back. Then John waited,
wondering how Danny would see anything if the fog didn't
clear. And if the fog got worse, maybe they would never
find their way out of the woods at all . . . He made himself
stop worrying, but he couldn't stop being afraid. He petted
Ahab for a while and talked to him, wishing that Ahab
could talk back. Twice he heard Danny shout, but he
couldn't understand what it was he said. He yelled, "What!"
but there was no answer, and that worried him too.

135

The minutes passed slowly. John kept waiting and hoping for Danny to all at once drop down out of the tree beside him, to say that he'd seen the trail clearly from up there. But Danny didn't appear. John threw pebbles at a bush and talked to Ahab some more. Then there was another shout from up above—a couple of words. But the only one John could understand was the single word, "Stuck!"

He yelled, "What!" again anyway, hoping that he hadn't heard right.

"I'm stuck!" Danny yelled back down. He sounded a long way off, almost as Mr. Deener had sounded from up on top of his moon ladder.

John sat for a moment, trying to think. But now he couldn't think. There was nothing to think about. That's what his brain told him. He had to climb the tree. He had offered to climb the tree once, of course, but now he knew that he hadn't meant it. He had known that Danny would want to, that Danny was a better climber. There was no choice now, though. Danny *had* climbed it, and had somehow got stuck.

John stood up, told Ahab to stay where he was, and pulled himself into the lower branches of the tree. The bark was hard and slick, but there were hand-holds in the trunk, and the limbs were close enough together so that he could work his way up from one to another. After climbing a bit, he looked down through the branches and fog and there was Ahab, far below, looking up at him. Quickly John looked away, grabbing the tree trunk and hanging on. He was already awfully high. At least the fog was thinner now.

He shouted at Danny to hang on, and then climbed higher, edging around the trunk of the tree, trying to see through the leafy curtain around him. A ghost of fog drifted through, but as John climbed higher, up into it, he saw that now and then the air was clear, that the fog was patchy, and was thin as often as it was thick.

Climbing was pretty easy in the lower limbs. He started to feel as if he was good t it. Soon, though, he was above most of the other trees, and the forest floor was nearly hidden to him. He was so far above the ground that he

didn't dare look down again. Slowly he looked up. It felt to him as if raising his head might throw him over backward, and he realized that his legs were shaking. Now that he had stopped and thought about it, climbing all of a sudden didn't seem easy any more. But there was Danny. John could see him now. He was way up above, where the trunk of the tree turned into a sort of Y. "Hey!" John shouted. "Wait!"

"What do you mean, 'wait'?" Danny shouted back down at him.

That was a good question, but John didn't bother thinking about it. Later, when they were safe on the ground, it might seem like a funny thing to have said. Right now it didn't seem funny. John reached for the next branch, but it was just too high. He could touch it, but he couldn't grab it. He scrabbled with his foot to find some place to push himself up, but then he realized that if he did manage to pull himself onto the next branch, he mightn't get back down. That was the way with tree climbing. It was getting down that was the trouble, when you couldn't see the little bits of broken limbs or the knots in the trunk that you had seen so easily when climbing up. He could imagine himself slipping, losing his grip and sliding off through the branches, rushing through the air. He hugged the trunk and shut his eyes, standing just like that until he could lower himself down to where he was sitting instead of standing, while all these terrible thoughts whispered through his head like goblin voices.

"What are you doing?" Danny shouted.

John forced himself to look around. The wind blew through his hair. There hadn't been any breeze down below, but higher up there was an ocean wind that jiggled the branches and rustled the leaves.

He waited, watching. The air was grey with fog suddenly, drifting on the sea wind. It didn't seem to come from the ocean, though. It came from deeper into the woods, from where the goblin fire still burned among the dark trees. Then once more the fog cleared, as if someone had opened a window in it. The full moon looked down from the sky. The breeze pushed the curtain of leaves aside, and through the clearing he saw the ocean and long green waves rolling in through dark rocks.

Then there was fog again, and the view of the ocean was gone. He pointed to where it had been, and, very slowly and carefully, he looked up. "There's the ocean," he shouted at Danny. "Straight out in the direction of that big, twisted limb."

Danny didn't say anything. He could see it too, of course, better than John. After a moment he said, "Are you stuck, too?"

"No," John said. "Just resting." He felt as if he were frozen there. If he moved in either direction, to climb farther up or to start back down, he would slide straight off the limb. He had been able to climb up there, of course, but suddenly that didn't make any difference to him. He simply couldn't move, and he steadied himself against the trunk, waiting. As he waited he began to think again.

First he wondered almost happily whether Mrs. Barlow and Polly might not be coming along at any moment. Perhaps he would see them on the trail, and he and Danny could shout in order to get their attention. But what would Mrs. Barlow do? Climb the tree and carry him down? Throw him a doughnut?

And what was Mr. Jimmers doing in the meantime? That was the real problem. If they were going to get home at all—not to Aunty Flo's house, but back to their own house on Pine Street—then they would have to rescue Mr. Deener from himself. They couldn't do that if they were stuck in a tree. He bit his lip and studied the tree roundabout him.

"You okay?" Danny asked, and the tone of his voice made it clear that he was afraid, too, afraid that John wasn't anything like okay.

John pulled himself up. He scraped up and down with his foot, edging around until he found a foothold in the trunk. Carefully he pushed himself toward the limb above until he was holding onto it with his arms and elbows. He kicked and pulled, yanking himself higher, getting his knee over it finally and sitting up. The branch above that one was easy. He could step right up onto it. And then there was another that ran alongside it. He edged out onto it, holding on to a

138

limb, and stepped across onto a crooked branch that was shaped almost like a hand. There were plenty of little limbs tangled together there, and it felt safe and solid.

There was Danny, straight above him, not eight feet away. He had one foot in a hole in the trunk and was holding onto a couple of little swelled-up places that had grown where limbs had broken off clean. His upper leg was caught in the crotch where the trunk split and angled off in two directions. He was jammed down in there tight. The little bumps that Danny held onto weren't nearly good enough hand-holds for him to pull himself up and out, and he couldn't touch the limb below his free foot, either. It was a yard out of reach.

"Here I am," John said. And then, trying to make Danny feel better, he said, "This looks easy."

It didn't, though, but there was nothing to do about that. John climbed across to the limb below Danny, the one Danny couldn't reach. "Step on my shoulder," John said, and hunched down, grabbing the trunk to hold on. "Where were you going, to the moon?"

"The fog was too thick," Danny said. "I was trying to get above it, but I got stuck here and couldn't go up or down." He stepped on John's shoulder, and John stood up part way, so that Danny could push good and hard. With something to push against, Danny was able to yank his leg out of the crotch of the tree, and after a moment of resting, he lowered himself down to John's limb, and together they climbed back down to the hand-shaped branch, where there was plenty of room to sit and rest.

The air was clear and clean way up there, although there was still fog down below. There lay the ocean, distant and green. And there, high above the edge of the forest, was the house on the hill, maybe two or three miles away. They couldn't see their trail. It hadn't been wide enough. From that distance it was lost in the undergrowth. They couldn't see Ahab below, either. The fog along the ground was too heavy. They looked way down through the branches until they found one that pointed in the direction of the house. It had been broken off, too. They would be able to recognize it from the ground, if the fog wasn't too thick.

John could have sat up there for hours, just the two of them, looking at the countryside around them. He wished they had a few of Mrs. Barlow's doughnuts to eat. He realized suddenly why he was so happy and content to sit there. It was because he had done what he had to do, even though he had been afraid to, and he had done it pretty well.

Now he had to climb down, of course. But as long as he sat there looking around, then he was doing something besides climbing down, and right at the moment that made him happy enough.

In the windy silence, though, they heard the piping of willow flutes and the distant bonging of a deep drum. The sounds reminded John that there were goblins in the woods, and that reminded him that they still had to find Mr. Deener—and soon, too. There was nothing to do but climb down now. Waiting wouldn't make it any easier.

They went about it slowly. They studied out the limb below, and John edged down to where he could grab onto a smaller branch before lowering himself. Then he worked his way back in toward the trunk, and there, two or three feet below him, was a hole where a limb had long ago fallen off, and there was a little jagged edge to put his shoe against. He slid his tennis shoe into it and carefully slid off his limb, down toward the next one.

Danny followed along right behind, and once, when Danny couldn't quite reach the next branch down, John grabbed his ankle and guided him down to it. In some ways it was easier than he thought it would be. He was awfully far from the ground, and that made it harder, but then he had company, and that helped. When he looked up, he could see how far they had come, and suddenly he was sure that they would make it. Just keep going, he said to himself. One branch after another. He looked down then and saw Ahab's face turned up toward him, and after a couple more minutes of easy climbing he was hugging Ahab around the neck.

They sat down at the base of the tree to rest for just a second. John's legs were still shaking, as if he had the shivers, so he slapped his knees and told them to keep still.

Danny laughed with relief and hit John on the shoulder. Then he pointed into the sky, where the fog had cleared again and the moon shone through, looking for all the world as if it had a face on it, and was keeping a careful eye on them. John jumped up and pointed into the tree. "That twisted limb way up there points toward the ocean," he said.

Danny looked up into the branches. "And there's the broken branch," he said, "the one that points toward the house."

"So what do you think?" asked John. "I say the trail is over there." And he pointed away to the right.

"Sure," Danny said. "Let's go."

"Wait," John said. "We'll find a branch that's in between the other two branches. Then we'll line it up with three more trees, say, and then walk to the second tree and line the third tree up with two more. We'll go straight on that way, and not around in circles, and sooner or later we've got to hit Mr. Deener's path again."

They were off at once, before the fog got too thick for them to do all the lining up and the searching for trees. They hadn't gone fifty feet before they found the little game trail that led to the path they had first followed into the woods. It was plain as day now. Ahab trotted away up the trail without stopping to think, and the boys followed him, trusting his nose.

In five minutes they were at Mr. Deener's path again, and hurrying along toward the sea. Time was wasting.

CHAPTER SIXTEEN

THE HOUSE OF DREAMS

Within ten minutes they were walking along the top of a cliff over the ocean. Mr. Deener's path wound around the shoreline, out onto a seaside meadow that was wet with misty air. The fog wasn't so bad anymore. It was as if the ocean wind had blown most of it into the woods, or as if there hadn't ever been any proper fog at all. Maybe it had been a goblin trick, like the dancing fire.

The moon shined overhead again, as if it were painted on the air, and the sun was a white glow out over the sea. On the meadow a yellow and white wooden house sat in the grass and wildflowers.

It was their own house, back on Pine Street. Only there was no Pine Street, no street at all. There was just the house sitting there all alone with the garage behind it, and a front walk that led nowhere.

Ahab yipped twice and ran toward it as if he thought he were home. When he got to the front walk, though, he stopped, skidding on all four paws so that he nearly fell on his nose. He sniffed around, back and forth, searching, maybe, for Penny the cat, or for the smell of something familiar.

After a moment he stopped sniffing and crept slowly back to where John and Danny still stood. They could see that it wasn't their house, not really; it was Mr. Deener's house. The carport hadn't been built yet. Mrs. Owlswick's window hadn't been put in. The front door was different.

The whole house was different. There was something strange about it. Misty light swirled around, as if ghosts were circling it, trying to get in at the windows. And the windows themselves seemed one moment to be glass, with moonlight shining off the panes, and the next moment to be dark, empty air, like the shadows of windows. There were lights on inside, and two people moving around. Smoke tumbled up out of the chimney like steam out of a pipe.

John and Danny walked across the meadow, around the house. Straightaway they found six of Mrs. Barlow's china plates, lined up together. They followed the ray of moonlight that glowed through them, and found the first of several jars of glass chips. Behind the house lay a big knapsack and two baskets. Jars of ocean water sat side by side on top of the overturned baskets. Rays of moonlight bounced in and out through the water, shooting off in a dozen directions toward the edges of the house and toward the roof.

There were mirrors on the meadow too, and bottles of green tea. There were glowing jars bound up in ivy leaves, full of moonstones and water. There were oyster shells polished very thin, and spiral seashells with the tips cut off, so that moonlight was funnelled through the big end, spinning around and around and out the hole at the tiny end, straight through a big, curved piece of green bottle glass, and so on and so on. There was a spinning maze of moonlight, all reflected and filtered in a thousand directions.

The house wasn't built of wood and nails; it was nothing but moonlight and memories. It was a house built of glass magic.

And there was something more wrong with the house besides the shadowy windows. There were parts missing. At the corner of the house in back, where it ran up to the roof, there was nothing but a jumble of shadow. The yellow boards faded into misty nothing, as if Mr. Deener, maybe, couldn't quite remember what the house had looked like right at that spot.

The chimney wasn't all there either. You could see that from behind the house. And there was something wrong

144

with the brickwork around the back porch, too. The shape wasn't right, or else the pattern of the bricks was wrong, or something. And they weren't solid bricks. Instead, like the windows, they were the ghosts of bricks, and when you turned your head, and looked at them edgewise, you could see right through them.

"Well," said Danny, "what do we do?"

John shrugged. "We knock on the door. We have to."

"What do we say? Maybe we should pretend to be selling newspapers."

"We'll think of something. I bet he'll be happy to see us. He thinks he's gotten home again. Wait and see. He'll be a happy man now, especially when he sees the cookies." John didn't really believe this, but he wanted to very badly.

They walked back around to the front and stepped up onto the porch. They both felt dizzy for a moment, as if they had just been spinning around and had stopped. The concrete underneath their feet didn't feel much like concrete. It felt airy, like soft styrofoam. When John knocked, they could hear the knocking easily enough, but John could barely feel the door against his knuckles. The wood was almost papery, as if it had been mostly eaten by termites. It looked enough like a door, though.

It swung open and there stood Mr. Deener. It took him a moment to recognize them. But then he said, "Boys, boys, boys. Come in. You've come to pay us a visit." He didn't smile, and he didn't look like a happy man.

"If that's all right," said Danny. "We were just out taking a walk and . . ."

"First rate," Mr. Deener said, and he motioned them in.

Ahab wouldn't follow. They called him and waved their arms, but he turned right around, trotted down the two steps onto the walk, and stepped off onto the grass, where he lay down to wait.

Both John and Danny wished that they were waiting out on the grass with Ahab. They could see Mrs. Deener in the kitchen, moving back and forth. She didn't seem to know they were there. She wore an apron and carried a wooden spoon.

The furniture was covered with doilies, and there were

flowers in a vase on the table. They weren't any kind of flowers that John had seen before, though, and when he sniffed them, they didn't smell like anything at all. Up close they looked as if they were made from cobweb or had been spun out of moonlight. Almost nothing in the house was really solid or was quite the right colour. It was a ghost house, through and through, and it was dim and dark, like an old memory.

Mr. Deener sat in a big, comfortable-looking chair. It seemed real enough. Maybe that was because he had known it so well. He had sat in it ten thousand times, so he remembered it particularly clearly. His eyes stared out the window, toward the sea. He wore a sweater, which was good, because the walls of the house didn't keep the sea breeze out very well at all. After a moment the boys realized that he wasn't going to say anything.

"So you've moved out here?" John said, giving Danny a look, although he said it to Mr. Deener.

"I've moved back home," said Mr. Deener. He said it in a flat sort of voice, almost an echo. There didn't seem to be anything much to him. He was like the flowers on the table. He had the appearance of Mr. Deener, but everything that ought to have been inside him had gone somewhere else—to make the goblins, maybe, and the henny-pennies.

Mrs. Deener came in just then. She was very pleasant looking and smiling, but she didn't seem to see John and Danny at all. It was as if they weren't there. Mr. Deener took the plate of food she gave him and said thank you, and then he put it down on the little table next to his chair. It was pork chops and mashed potatoes and gravy and cauliflower, with gravy on it too. All of it was sort of white.

Mrs. Deener went out, back into the kitchen, and Mr. Deener watched her go. He had such a far away look in his eyes that he might just as easily have been looking at the moon. He seemed rooted into his chair, too. He picked up his plate and forked up a bite of potatoes, but when he got it outside his mouth, it was gone—just like that, into nothing. He nodded, though, as if he liked the mouthful of air that he had eaten, and he took another bit of nothing. He had the look on his face of someone who hadn't eaten in

146

ten years, but who had suddenly remembered how food used to taste.

He cleaned his plate that way. When he was done there wasn't even a spot of gravy left. It was cleaner even than if Ahab had been at it. Mrs. Deener came back in and took the plate away, and Mr. Deener said the food was "delicious." Then he went back to staring out the window.

"Going to stay out here, then?" asked John.

Mr. Deener sat staring, his mind gone to the moon. "Out here?" he asked after a moment. He didn't seem to know what John meant. "I'm home," he said. "I've come home to stay."

"Mrs. Barlow has sent you these cookies," Danny said. He opened his backpack and took them out.

"Mrs. Barlow," said Mr. Deener, as if he barely remembered Mrs. Barlow, maybe from a dream.

"Yes," John said. "She's been baking all day today—pies, cakes, doughnuts, cookies." This part wasn't entirely true, of course, but John wanted to see what Mr. Deener would do when he heard such a thing. "Why don't you come on up to the house for a bite of dessert?"

He didn't say anything for a long minute. Then he said, "I . . . I used to like a cookie," but he didn't take one. Finally Danny offered one to John, and the boys ate the six cookies themselves. Mrs. Deener brought in another plate of food and went out again, standing for a moment in the doorway, still holding her wooden spoon.

The meadow outside brightened just a little right then, and thin rays of sunlight slanted through the window behind her. For a moment she grew cloudy and watery, like ice. They could see the kitchen counters through her, and they could see the wall of the house through the kitchen counters. And through the wall of the house they could see the meadow and the oak woods far beyond.

Mrs. Deener and the house were built out of layers and layers of nothing—of ghosts. And Mr. Deener wanted to live among them. John didn't want to live among them, not for another moment. It was his house, too, and Danny's. It was the ghost of a house that would one day be theirs. They didn't want to think of living in a house that was all shadows and moonlight. It was frightening, like being out of doors at midnight. There was something in the air that didn't have anything to do with their house at all, and it gave John the creeps.

He was sure, somehow, that it didn't have very much to do with the house Mr. Deener used to live in either. It was the memory of the house, and a kind of a patchwork memory, too. But Mr. Deener didn't know that, because he had used his glass magic to give away all the little bits of him that had let him know anything at all.

"Let's go for a walk along the cliffs," Danny said, maybe thinking that it would be good just to get Mr. Deener out of there.

He wouldn't budge, though.

"Mrs. Deener could come along," said John. "Maybe she would like to come up to Aunty Flo's for dessert."

Mr. Deener seemed to be made of stone. When they mentioned Mrs. Deener, they might as well have said nothing at all. She still moved about in the kitchen. They could hear the sound of running water and of plates clanking together in the sink.

"We were hoping to have another go at the moon ladder," Danny said. "Or maybe try something else. Maybe you could make a flying carpet or something, with glass balls and holly leaves and all."

Mr. Deener's eyes were shut. He was thinking very hard, remembering. Out in the kitchen, Mrs. Deener suddenly started to sing in an odd high-pitched voice. She got the words wrong, started over, and then got the words wrong again. Mr. Deener squished his face up, looking as if he were going to pop. Suddenly there was a furious clanking of dishes in the sink, as if an octopus were washing dishes, banging them all together at once. A tea kettle started to whistle. Pan lids rattled. Cupboard doors opened and closed with a bang. There was an orchestra of kitchen noises all at once.

Mr. Deener smashed himself into his chair, remembering harder and harder. All at once there was the smell of flowers in the room, and the bouquet on the table stirred just a little. John could recognize the different flowers all of

148

a sudden. Somehow, though, their being more real was worse than their being nothing but a trick of moonlight. The whole house was growing more solid. Colours were brightening.

John and Danny got up to leave. The tea kettle screeched in the kitchen. They could hear heavy footsteps in the bedroom. It was Mrs. Deener in there too, moving around. There she was again, sewing something in the den. They could just see her past the edge of the door. She was here, she was there—flitting from one room to another like a goblin fire. The whole house, and Mr. Deener too, seemed ready to boil over. Mr. Deener wanted them out of there; John could feel it.

By the time they got to the front door, the smell of the flowers was fading, and the tea kettle only hissed. The kitchen fell silent. Mr. Deener stayed in his chair. He wasn't so awfully scrunched up any more, and he even waved just a little as they stepped out onto the porch. The only thing about their visit that had made him happy was their leaving again.

They could see him through the window, sitting there, half smiling, as the ghost of Mrs. Deener moved through the kitchen, putting together another plate of ghost food, singing half remembered songs.

CHAPTER SEVENTEEN

THE ARRIVAL OF POLLY AND MRS. BARLOW

There were henny-penny men hanging around with Ahab. The air was full of leaves. They flew around and around, as if they were trying to get into the house to yell at Mr. Deener, but they couldn't get past the slanting moonlight, the glass magic. They were trapped outside. Mr. Deener was safe from them at last. John wondered if he was safe from the goblins, too.

Then he stopped for a moment, right at the edge of the porch. He stood there thinking. "I've got an idea," he said.

"Good," said Danny, "because we can't help him by talking to him. What's your idea?"

"Come on," John said, and he set off around the house.

They found Mrs. Barlow's plates again, lined up one after another. John jumped on the first of them, cracking it in half. "Smash them up," he said, stomping it into pieces. "We've got to act like goblins."

"Why?" Danny stood there staring, as if John had gone nuts. John picked up the second plate and zingoed it off across the meadow, over the cliff, then kicked the third like a football. It broke to pieces in the air.

"We're going to wreck his house."

"Wreck his house? *That's* not going to make him happy."

"We don't want him happy. He gave happiness away to his goblins, along with all that other stuff. What we're going to do is get him out of there. It's the only way. Aunty Flo said that we didn't have to *tell* Mr. Deener anything. But

151

maybe we do. Maybe we have to yell in his ear and wake him up."

Danny picked up the last two plates and banged them together like cymbals. "Let's do it," he said.

They went after the bottles of ocean water next, pouring them out and putting the bottles back into one of the baskets. Then they threw the seashells all over the place. Then they gathered up the jars full of glass chips and put them in the basket. The henny-pennies sailed around cheering.

Ahab came running from the front yard. There were a dozen henny-pennies riding on his back. One rode on his head, steering him by pulling on his ears. They rode through a glass bowl full of green cheese, knocking it flying, then kicked over the jar full of moonstones. Some of the henny-pennies landed their leaves and picked up the little stones, which they threw at mirrors and pieces of bottle glass.

The web of moonlight that angled around the meadow shimmered and shuddered. Bit by bit the house was gone, like invisible ink drying and disappearing on a page. The chimney vanished, and the roof along with it. The garage blinked away. The windows were nothing but dark holes, and the wood siding on the house seemed to crumble into termite dust and blow away on the sea wind.

In the end, there was only Mr. Deener left, smashed into his favourite chair, holding onto the stuffed arms of the thing as if he were holding onto a rowboat on a tossing sea. The ghost of Mrs. Deener wandered back and forth where the kitchen had been. They could just hear the sound of her singing and the tooting of the tea kettle. All at once there was nothing left of her but an apron and a wooden spoon, floating over the meadow.

Then, poof, even those little bits of her were gone too, and Mr. Deener sat on top of a moss-covered rock in the grass. His eyes were still smashed shut.

"We should have saved him a cookie," Danny said.

John nodded. "He'll be hungry, I bet, after eating nothing but ghost food all morning. That would be like eating in a dream. You wake up hungry."

But Mr. Deener didn't want any cookies. He didn't seem to want anything at all except to sit there on the rock. Did he think he was still sitting in a chair? He wouldn't even open his eyes. At first it looked as if he had gone to sleep, like the Mr. Deener upstairs in the tower. But he hadn't done that either. He was just sort of frozen there with his eyes shut.

The henny-pennies were worked up from having helped wreck the house. They landed on Mr. Deener's shoulders and tugged on his ears. One of them climbed up onto his nose and pushed one of his eyelids open as if he were opening a garage door. Ahab licked his face.

"Mr. Deener!" John shouted.

He wouldn't budge.

The henny-pennies yammered in his ear. They had such tiny voices that John and Danny couldn't catch more than a word of it. Mr. Deener clapped his hands over his ears, nearly squashing one of the little men. He kept his hands there, pressing out the sound of their yelling.

Then they saw Polly running down the path out of the woods, carrying a basket. Mrs. Barlow puffed along behind, trying to keep up and with a fierce look on her face, as if she wasn't going to put up with any nonsense from anyone, especially Mr. Deener. They must have seen the house fly apart, because neither one of them seemed surprised to see the mess of baskets and bottles and jars and Mr. Deener sitting on his rock.

"Aunty Flo is down on the meadow," Polly said to them, "near the window. She's got the Sleeper with her. We lugged him down there on the wagon; that's why we took so long to get here. What's going on? Why is Mr. Deener sitting here with his eyes shut?"

"He'd built himself a house out of glass magic," John said. "So we tore it down."

"It's nearly wrecked him, too," Danny said.

"*Wrecked* him?" Mrs. Barlow said. "Deener doesn't know from wrecked. *I'll* wreck him to pieces if he doesn't look sharp." She pinched him on the arm then—not hard, but enough to make him jump. "This one here is coming along to the meadow, too," she said. "It's time we put an end to his foolishness."

"He sure doesn't *want* to come," said Danny. "He won't do anything but sit here."

Mrs. Barlow shook her head. "You boys stand back. I'll cook his goose for him. He's a good man, one of the best. I won't let him play himself false. Deener!" she shouted, as close as she could get to his ear.

The henny-pennies swarmed around, shouting "Deener! Deener! Deener!" John could just barely hear them, like the piping little voices of tiny frogs. Mr. Deener ignored them all. He might as well have been made of chalk and paint.

Polly opened her basket and pulled out a glazed doughnut, puffy and sugary and smelling as if it had just that moment come out of the oven, which it couldn't have. She smiled at John and Danny. "Food magic," she said, holding it in Mr. Deener's face and whispering into his ear.

He shuddered, as if a tiny earthquake had shaken him. His nose twitched. He pried open one eye and looked at the doughnut. Then he shut it again. What he wanted, maybe, was another plate of ghost food. The ghost of Mrs. Deener was gone, though, and her kitchen was gone with it. Mrs. Barlow gave him a push on the shoulder. "*Would* you get up?" she said.

He shook his head.

Polly waved the doughnut at him again, right under his nose, and his head moved back and forth just a little, following it. The henny-pennies rode past, reaching out and pulling little hunks out of the doughnut, eating it in front of his face, rubbing their stomachs and making contented noises. Mr. Deener opened his eyes then. One of the little men snatched up a big piece of doughnut with both hands and threw it to Ahab, and then pulled off another piece and shoved it onto his head like a hat.

Mr. Deener was furious suddenly, and he pulled the rest of the doughnut out of Polly's hand and shoved it into his mouth. Then he closed his eyes again, sitting there as ever, not even chewing it up. Mrs. Barlow glared at him. "Eat the doughnut!" she said.

Mr. Deener wouldn't eat it.

"Chew it up!"

He shook his head.

154

Mrs. Barlow took his nose in one hand and his chin in the other and wiggled them back and forth and up and down. Mr. Deener swatted the air, as if she were a bothersome fly. The henny-pennies flew in and tried to help, tugging this way and that way on Mr. Deener's nose.

"Enough!" Mr. Deener shouted suddenly. Then he chewed up the doughnut and swallowed it. "There!" he said. "Leave a man alone."

"Up you go," Mrs. Barlow said, grabbing his arm. "Give him a push, Polly. Get around behind him there. You boys latch onto his sweater or something."

John grabbed his other arm and Danny took hold of his belt. Together they pulled and pushed him to his feet. "Let's take him down to the ocean," Mrs. Barlow said, winking at the boys. "Let's throw him in. Cold salt water will wake him up!"

"No!" shouted Mr. Deener. And Polly shoved the edge of another doughnut into his open mouth.

"That's right, Mr. Deener, take a bite." Mrs. Barlow said, patting him on the back happily. "We won't pitch you into the sea if you have a nice bite of glazey."

He took his bite, but pretended not to like it. He screwed his face up and swallowed it hard, as if the doughnut were made out of something awful. "It's a dirt cutlet," he said.

"That's right, Deener," Mrs. Barlow and Polly pulled him along down the path. Now that he was up off his rock, it wasn't too hard to make him go. "Come along nice or we'll feed you a toad pie. We're on our way home now. You might as well get used to the idea."

"Home," said Mr. Deener, but he was thinking of the past.

John was thinking of the spectacles. They still weren't whole. Even if they could get Mr. Deener back through the woods, what good would it do them? His glass magic hadn't worked to get them home. It hadn't worked to get anyone home, except Mr. Deener. And that kind of a home was worse than no home at all.

No, it was time to think about the spectacles. John took them out of his jacket and said, "Danny and I have to be getting along. We have to find the lens to these spectacles.

The goblins stole it, and we've got to get it back if we want to go home. We don't think Mr. Deener can get us there with his jars of broken glass."

Mrs. Barlow nodded. "Mr. Deener can't get across the street with his jars of glass," she said. "The only thing he can get is into trouble. But his way and your way are the same. They both lead through the woods, and we're all going home through the same window, if you don't mind. We'll find the lens of the Moon Man's spectacles along the way, even if we have to turn every goblin in the woods upside down. You know where the goblins came from. They're part of Mr. Deener. They *are* Mr. Deener. He's like a magnet, Mr. Deener is. He'll fetch his goblins to us, and we'll make them give over what isn't theirs. Pick up some of that trash, will you boys?"

The henny-penny men seemed happy at this news. They flew around and around on their leaves in a sort of wind devil, and then scoured away toward the oak woods, rising and falling on the sea wind. Ahab ran after them, barking.

John and Danny hurried around, filling Mr. Deener's knapsack with the junk that lay about the meadow. They didn't bother with the seashells or the green cheese, but they picked up the rest of the jars and the broken plates and empty bottles. They left the basket for squirrels to live in, and ran along down the path toward where Mrs. Barlow and Polly were just then towing Mr. Deener into the shadow of the woods. When the boys caught up with them, Mrs. Barlow made Mr. Deener wear the backpack. "He hauled this trash out here," she said. "He can haul it back. We've got to work on his appetite."

Mr. Deener stumbled along. He pretended to have his eyes shut, but Danny could see that he was peeking just a little bit, so that he wouldn't trip and hurt himself on the rough path. He was moaning, too, and mumbling things. Polly did her best to help him out, warning him about branches and holes and trying to talk him into another doughnut.

He was different, though, than he had been when he was sitting in his chair in his ghost house. He had been empty there—almost a ghost himself. But now, in the sea wind

156

and with Mrs. Barlow tugging him along and Polly being nice to him, he was Mr. Deener again, although he was pretending very hard not to be.

He wouldn't look at Polly's doughnut, but when she put it away again, he opened his eyes and peeked at the open basket. Then, twenty steps farther on, he said, "Maybe just a little nibble."

Polly gave him the doughnut. "Here's the biggest one," she said.

"Still warm!" He held it up happily, nodding at it.

Polly gave him a squeeze on the arm. "Food magic," she said, "Thanks to Mrs. Barlow."

He smiled at that and ate his doughnut.

Somehow, the sight of Mr. Deener eating a doughnut cheerfully was far more wonderful than John or Danny would have thought. They almost wanted to cheer. Maybe it was because they liked Mr. Deener, and Mr. Deener always seemed happiest when he had something nice to eat; maybe it was because ghosts eat ghost food, and an hour ago it had seemed as if Mr. Deener had magicked all the life out of himself until he had become a ghost. But now here he was, getting his appetite back, eating a jolly doughnut.

He kept one eye open now—the one on the other side of his head from where Mrs. Barlow walked. That way he could pretend still to have them shut. He was only playing at being sorrowful, and that was a good sign.

The woods were dark, though, and the fog rose around them again. Mr. Deener began to look into the woods, as if he were worried. He didn't bother pretending anymore. Mrs. Barlow went straight along, also looking off through the trees. Polly held Mr. Deener's hand, but she didn't have to tow him along. John and Danny watched for the goblin fire. Ahab and the henny-pennies went along ahead, but not so far ahead that the boys couldn't see them.

They were a good way from the ocean when goblin laughter sounded, way off through the trees. They could still hear the crash of ocean waves, but at the same time came the sound of a drum being struck, like someone beating on a hollow tree, and the piping of willow flutes.

157

There was the fire, far off among the trees, burning in a small grassy clearing.

Then, suddenly, it was closer. Just like that. Earlier that morning, the fire had leaped away from them, leading them deeper into the woods. Now it seemed to be leaping closer, as if it were drawn to Mr. Deener. Again it winked out and then in a moment winked back on—now away to the right, toward the ocean, now off to the left, almost lost in a thicket of oak scrub. All at once it lay straight in front of them, burning and crackling and throwing long shadows across the tree trunks.

They could see goblins dancing around the fire, playing flutes. Their hair was wild about their heads. There was a lot of yelling, too, and fighting and pushing. Two or three goblins sat off by themselves with their noses in the air, as if they were refusing to mingle with the others. One stood on a fallen log, gobbling out a lot of goblin talk, but no one paid him any attention until someone hit him in the face with a fish. Then all the goblins laughed and pointed.

They had a great black kettle on the fire, bubbling away. One of them picked the fish up out of the dirt and threw it into the kettle. Another pulled one of the jewelled pins from his bat vest and threw that in too.

The kettle steamed and bubbled. A great cloud of fog poured out of it, into the trees. So it wasn't an ocean fog at all that lay over the woods. It was steam from the kettle—more of Mr. Deener's magic. There was a shape in the fog, a circle of misty white that hung over the mouth of the kettle. It was the reflection of the full moon, which must have hung in the sky above the clearing, although you couldn't see it because of the fog.

Mrs. Barlow looked grim. The henny-pennies sailed around in the air, watching. Everyone was being very quiet, sneaking up. John wondered what they meant to do. There wasn't anything to be gained by beating the goblins up or something. What was needed was to make the glasses whole again.

Mr. Deener had a faint smile on his face, like the smile of a father watching his children play, or of an artist happy with one of his own paintings. Mrs. Barlow stood just

158

behind him, with her hand on his back now. She gestured at Polly to drop Mr. Deener's hand, which she did.

Where would the glasses be? Buried somewhere? In the pocket of a bat shirt? What if the goblins had smashed them up, just for fun?

That didn't seem likely. Somehow it seemed as if the goblins wanted the spectacles, maybe to do their own sort of glass magic. Why not? They were a lot of little Mr. Deeners, weren't they? If the spectacles were whole then the goblins could see Mrs. Owlswick's window and could climb straight into John and Danny's bedroom, out the front door of the house, and into the neighbourhood. John remembered the picture in the water of the fountain—the picture of the house all dusty and gone to sleep . . .

They had to find the missing lens, and right now.

One of the goblins rooted around in the pile of glass jewelry, clutching two handfuls and dumping them into the pot. Fog boiled out again, away into the woods. Maybe the lens was in that heap of jewelry. Maybe . . . John looked at the kettle. What happened to the jewelry when it fell into the misty kettle? Did it melt? Turn to fog?

"The kettle," John said to Danny. "It's in the kettle. It must be. Let's go."

But just then, before they'd had time to go anywhere, Mrs. Barlow pushed Mr. Deener hard. He stumbled out into the clearing, waving his arms wildly, straight into the middle of the dancing goblins.

CHAPTER EIGHTEEN

THE END OF THE GOBLINS

Surprised and shouting, Mr. Deener caught himself and stood up straight, trying to look very stern, as if he had *meant* to come rushing out of the bushes like that. He didn't much know what to say or do, though, so he turned around and looked at Mrs. Barlow. He shrugged his shoulders as if he was mad at her for pushing him. Mrs. Barlow waved her hand at him and then waved it at the goblins. Polly nodded. So he coughed once, very loud, and said to the goblins, "See here!"

He could hardly be heard above the noise. As soon as he had rushed in among them, the goblins had begun to laugh and shout and carry on. They danced around him and tugged at his clothes. They leaped up to try to pull his hair. Two of them found an old rusty iron bowl and scooped a lot of steaming fish muck out of the kettle. They brought it to him happily, and one of the goblins dipped his hand into the bowl and pulled out an old fish skeleton, shoving it dripping into Mr. Deener's pants pocket. The rest of the goblins laughed and laughed.

"You're awful!" he shouted at them, knocking the bowl out of their hands. "Awful, awful, awful!" He yanked out the fish skeleton and threw it onto the ground, and four or five goblins made a rush for it, as if it were a treasure.

"The spectacles, Mr. Deener!" Polly shouted at him. "Find the missing lens!"

"Miss Polly would like the spectacles to be whole again,"

Mr. Deener said to the goblins. He was very calm about it, very polite. The goblins only laughed louder. One of them climbed onto another one's shoulders and played a flute straight into Mr. Deener's face. Others began to throw leaves and twigs and dirt at him. One snatched Mr. Deener's pocket watch out of his vest pocket and threw it into the kettle.

Mr. Deener put his hands over his face and turned to run. He couldn't stand any more torment. The henny-pennies flew at him just then, though, and drove him back into the clearing. They chased him this way and that way while the goblins gobbled with laughter and poked and pinched, hanging onto his pockets and trying to climb up onto his back. Around and around the clearing he ran, through the misty air. And every time he tried to get free of them, to crash away into the forest and escape, the henny-pennies chased him back.

He stopped, finally, breathing hard, but the goblins still didn't leave him alone. He swatted at them and yelled at them, but they didn't care. One of them tied his shoelaces together while the other goblins poked him in the stomach with bony fingers. He caught his breath finally and pushed them away. Then he straightened his vest, trying to look dignified. He set out to walk back to where Polly and Mrs. Barlow stood. "I tried," he said. "No one can accuse me . . ." But then he tripped on his tied-up shoelaces and sprawled on his face in the weeds.

"Don't be such a panty-waist!" Mrs. Barlow shouted.

The goblins roared and hooted. They had him then. John and Danny could see that. The goblins climbed up onto Mr. Deener's back and began pulling his hair and stuffing cooked fish down his collar. The boys jumped out and ran toward Mr. Deener. Ahab wanted to follow along, but Mrs. Barlow held onto him. "This is the Deener's fight," she said to Ahab, and then she shouted at John and Danny, "Gettum boys!" but it wasn't clear who or what she wanted them to get.

Polly ran out to help Mr. Deener. Four goblins sat on his back as if he were a horse. They kicked at him and pulled his hair. "Go! Go!" they seemed to be shouting. She pulled two of them off, and Mr. Deener rolled heavily onto his back, smashing the two that were still hanging on.

What John and Daniel wanted was the lens. It was there somewhere; it must be. The heap of jewelry was a good place to start, and if it wasn't there they would try the kettle. They would help Mr. Deener and Polly, too, in a moment. But the goblins hadn't really been hurting Mr. Deener so much as tormenting him, and since the goblins were his fault anyway, he would just have to put up with a little tormenting.

Mr. Deener stumbled halfway to his feet, though, still trying to get at his shoelaces. "Hold still for a moment!" Polly shouted at him. But he wouldn't hold still. He kicked through the pile of jewelry on the ground, knocking it around. Goblins rushed in, holding onto his suspenders now, pulling and snapping them and poking him in the ribs. "Ow! Ow!" Mr. Deener cried, batting them away. He was in a fury. His face was the colour of a red cabbage. Polly worked at the shoe laces, trying to get the knot out.

Mr. Deener couldn't stand it any longer, though. He lunged at one of the worst of the goblins, trying to catch it by the vest. "Got them!" Polly shouted, meaning the shoe laces, and she jumped up and out of Mr. Deener's way.

There was a furious barking just then. Mrs. Barlow had let Ahab loose, and he rushed in to help, going after the same goblin that Mr. Deener wanted. Mr. Deener fell straight over Ahab's back. He grabbed hold of the goblin to stop himself, and the three of them—Ahab, Mr. Deener, and the goblin—tumbled forward and slammed against the big kettle, which rocked back and forth, tilting dangerously.

Steaming water splashed out all over John, who shouted out loud, thinking that the water would burn him. It was cold water, though, like ocean water. The fire under the kettle was cold, too, or rather it felt like nothing at all. What it looked like, from up close, was cobweb and moonlight, just like the vase of flowers on the table in Mr. Deener's house of dreams.

The fight was raging around the kettle now, and Mr. Deener smashed into it again, wrestling with half a dozen

163

goblins at once. With a wild laugh he picked one up and dropped it into the kettle, like a chicken into a soup.

"That's it, Deener!" shouted Mrs. Barlow from where she stood eating a doughnut. The henny-pennies had left Mr. Deener alone by now, too. They sailed around Mrs. Barlow, helping themselves to doughnuts and watching the fight. This was what they wanted—Mr. Deener fighting back, paying out the goblins for all their mischief. Of course it was really Mr. Deener's mischief. He was cleaning up the bits and pieces of himself that had been broken up, just as the henny-pennies had cleaned up the broken glass from the moon ladder in the laboratory.

Mr. Deener went after the goblins like a wild man now, shouting threats and making the threats good. Danny and John dug through the high grass for the glasses lens. Polly went to help them, now that Mr. Deener was steamed up. They found no end of glass jewelry, of necklaces and rings and pins and bracelets. But there was no glasses lens.

A crowd of goblins smashed through, running from Mr. Deener. One snatched John's arm, holding onto his jacket, snaking his little hands into the pockets. Danny grabbed him and pulled him off, but two others leaped in to help, both of them making the glasses sign with their fingers. Polly fought with them, prying one of them off Danny's back.

Then Ahab appeared, barking and lunging, with Mrs. Barlow behind him. "It's late!" she shouted at Mr. Deener. "Time to quit this . . . Oof!" One of the goblins gave her apron a tug, nearly pulling her over.

Ahab picked it up by the bat vest, though, and hauled it away like a sack of dirt. The henny-pennies rode on Ahab's back, steering him around the clearing. They dumped the goblin at Mr. Deener's feet, and Mr. Deener pitched it into the kettle. The goblins were in a state now. They were laughing and brave when there was just Mr. Deener and Polly to fight with, but Ahab and Mrs. Barlow meant serious trouble. In twos and threes, goblins tried to sneak off into the trees, but Ahab and the henny-pennies would fetch them back every time, as if herding sheep.

The goblins were in a state. They raged around,

yammering and hooting and poking each other in the eye. They leaped at the foggy kettle to get a bit of fish to eat, and slapped each other with the bones or shoved them into their hair like combs. They wrestled and spit and howled. It didn't matter a bit to them who they were howling at. They didn't care who was who; they had simply run wild.

"The kettle!" John shouted. He waded toward it, with a goblin hanging around his waist. It had found the zippered pocket inside the jacket and was fumbling for it, trying to tug it open, to get at the spectacles. John grabbed the thing's arm and pulled, but the goblin hung on like a squid. Mrs. Barlow got hold of the thing's feet, and pulled, and Danny poked it under the arm pits until it howled and fell off.

John didn't want just to reach into the pot and stir things around. There was no telling what horrible things were in it. So he pushed on it instead, stepping right into the cold fire underneath. In an instant Polly stood next to him and pushed too. Both of them gave it a great heave, putting their shoulders into it.

The goblin that had been holding onto John grabbed him again. It shrieked and pulled, trying to drag him away now, to stop him from tipping over the kettle, which swung wildly, splashing water six feet into the air, drowning the ghost of the moon that still floated above it. One moment the moon was there, hovering in the fog, and the next moment the air was washed clean of it, like dirt off a window.

The wild fighting in the clearing stopped while everyone watched. The kettle began to shake as it swung. It wasn't shaking just because it had been given a knock; it was shaking all on its own, as if alive and dreadfully cold. John and Danny and Polly backed farther away, afraid of the magic, but the goblins stood stony still, frozen with fear.

Then, in a crowd, the goblins ran to the kettle and tried to steady it. It swung more and more wildly with each swing, sloshing back and forth, spilling out water, rocking and creaking and knocking goblins over like bowling pins.

"Look out!" shouted Mr. Deener as the kettle smashed down onto the ground, pouring out into the fire and weeds.

Ahab barked and danced around the fallen kettle. The goblins rushed at it, trying to haul it back up, trying to save some of the water and fishbones, throwing pieces of jewelry back into the little bit of water that was left. Suddenly Mr. Deener tried to help them. He had a surprised and frightened look on his face. He snatched up two handfuls of jewelry and cried, "Wait! Wait!" But there was nothing to wait for. There was no fire anymore, and no steam. The magic had drowned itself.

In a few moments the air was clear of fog. It was gone, just like that. When the last of the water had soaked into the ground, the last little ghosts of mist disappeared from the air. And as they did, the tip-top branches of trees grew clear and bright, and the clearning was washed in sunlight. All at once, the goblins standing roundabout the fallen kettle began to disappear too. Like Mrs. Deener in the house over the ocean, they grew watery and thin, and the boys could see straight through them. Then they were gone, just like that and all was silent except for the sound of distant sea waves.

Mr. Deener looked dizzy, as if he had been spinning around. He muttered something, maybe talking to someone that the rest of them couldn't see, or to someone inside his head. His face was full of emotions—of happiness and sorrow and fear and anger all at once, sort of shifting and changing until he covered his face with his hands and rubbed it, pulling at his nose and rubbing his eyes. He blinked a couple of times and then put his head over to the side as if to rattle something out of his ear.

The kettle lay in the grass, still shaking and shuddering. With a sound like ice breaking, it cracked and shivered into a thousand pieces. Then there was nothing left of the kettle at all. What lay on the grass were some old wire coathangers, a broken door knob, and a little heap of what looked like flakes of rust. Scattered around it were pieces of glass jewelry, and in among the jewelry lay the lost spectacles lens.

Mr. Deener grabbed for it, but Mrs. Barlow elbowed him aside and picked it up herself. "I believe this belongs to the boys," she said, and then handed it to John.

Mr. Deener made his smashed-up face, jamming his eyes shut. It wasn't a very good one, though. He didn't look as if he meant it, and when Polly ran across and found him a fresh doughnut in the basket, he ate it very happily. "Rough work," he said. "Builds up a man's hunger."

Mrs. Barlow gave Mr. Deener a little kiss on the cheek, and for a moment he looked even happier than when he'd eaten the doughnut. "We're proud of you," she said, "the way you went for those little men. They're gone now, all of them. Have something to eat."

Mr. Deener took another doughnut almost cheerfully. He looked different somehow, as if he no longer believed he was *poor* Mr. Deener, but was just plain Mr. Deener now. He wasn't as sickly looking, either—not nearly as pale. He looked tired but with a stout heart, like someone who has walked a long long way and is almost home.

Mrs. Barlow pulled a fish skeleton out of his vest pocket and threw it into the bushes. "Let's finish the job," she said.

This didn't make Mr. Deener look any happier, though. He squinted around the clearing. Then he looked at his hands. Then he put his hands over his eyes and stood very still, as if he were watching a movie on the backside of his eyelids. "I'm awfully hungry," he said suddenly, and he reached into Mrs. Barlow's basket for another doughnut.

Polly smiled at John and Danny and said, "Mr. Deener's got his appetite back."

"What happened to the henny-pennies?" Danny asked suddenly.

They were gone, all of them. Sycamore leaves lay scattered over the grass, but there wasn't a little man to be seen. Ahab seemed to be searching for them too, running around and sniffing at the fallen leaves.

Mrs. Barlow shrugged. "Went along with the goblins, I guess. Back to where they came from."

John looked at Mr. Deener. Were all the goblins and henny-pennies inside him now, in his head? Were the goblins all running around in there, causing trouble, while the henny-pennies yelled at him? As confusing as that might be, maybe that was better than being the sort of empty-headed ghost that Mr. Deener had slowly become.

John thought about his own goblins and henny-pennies. There were certainly a lot of them in there. Sometimes they were a troublesome crowd, but they were better than no company at all.

John pulled the spectacles out of his pocket and snapped the lens back into the rim, and then put them on and looked through them. The green woods were doubly green, but there was nothing magical to be seen.

"Be careful with them," Danny said. "Put them away."

John did. "You sound like a henny-penny man," he said, smiling at Danny. But Danny was right. This was no time to be trying the spectacles on. It was time for getting out to the meadow. Mrs. Barlow was already on her way along the path. She was chatting with Mr. Deener, who took her arm and called her "my dear."

"I think they're in love," Polly said happily.

In a half hour they were out of the woods.

CHAPTER NINETEEN

THROUGH THE BEDROOM WINDOW

There stood Aunty Flo, out on the meadow. The full moon sailed overhead, right next door to the sun. John pulled the spectacles out of his pocket straightaway. He couldn't wait. He was fearful, though, of what he would find. What if the window wasn't there? What if it had sailed away for good, and was simply gone? He looked through the spectacles at the moon first, which looked like nothing more than a great ball of green cheese with a face on it. What had Aunty Flo called him, the little man in the curiosity shop? Aiken Drum, just like in the G. Smithers book. It was *his* face on the moon.

So he looked at the pile of brush wood, and there hung the window, as ever. John shouted with joy, and Danny took the glasses from him so that he could see it too. Then they let Ahab have a glimpse through them, and off he went, running toward the window. Danny held onto the glasses, though, and when Ahab got to the heap of branches and put his paws up on them, of course he couldn't see anything at all. He stopped and sniffed around. Then he backed down onto the meadow grass and walked around the branches in a circle, sniffing and sniffing.

The boys ran toward him happily. It was high time they were getting home. There was no place they wanted to be more.

But there were Aunty Flo and Polly, waiting and watching, and Mr. Deener and Mrs. Barlow. Beside them, on a cart, lay the sleeping Mr. Deener, covered in a blanket, his head on a pillow. He slept as always—restless and muttering.

It seemed as if Mr. Deener couldn't quite bring himself to look at the sleeper. He looked in the other direction, toward the woods and the distant ocean. It was a faraway look, as if he could see the little house on the bluffs where he had lived just that morning with the ghost of his wife.

John and Danny had come to help, whether they wanted to help or not. They had gotten the job half done. They couldn't go home without finishing it. Danny stopped running toward the window, and a moment later John stopped too. He didn't want to stop. There was a goblin in him that told him to keep running, to climb in through the open window, help Ahab and Danny through, and pull the window closed after him. He didn't want to be off adventuring in magical lands and saving Mr. Deener from himself. He wanted to be home, shooting marbles in the backyard on a Sunday afternoon.

But he couldn't be. Not yet. There was a henny-penny man in him who told him that the adventure wasn't through. Mr. Deener wasn't put back together yet. He had got his own goblins and henny-penny men back, but that would only make him feel things more strongly again, and he would grow sorrowful and go to bits all over again. He had to be made whole. John and Danny had to finish the job. But how?

It was mostly up to Mr. Deener now. John put the spectacles on and looked at the man asleep. It wasn't Mr. Deener at all, not really—not any more than the fire in the clearing had been a real fire or the house on the bluffs had been a real house. It was a thing of magic. Through the spectacles John could see it for what it really was. It was just a bundle of straw and rags dressed up in Mr. Deener's clothes. Like the goblins and the moon ladder and the rest of Mr. Deener's magic, there was nothing to it but junk and foolery.

The straw man on the cart shifted and groaned, and Polly patted its head as if it were a real Mr. Deener. When John took the glasses off, of course, it *was* a real Mr. Deener again, or at least there was part of the real Mr. Deener in it.

"Does it still look like home?" asked Mrs. Barlow, pointing toward where the window hung.

"Just the same," said John. "Nothing's changed at all." He put his hand into his pocket just then, and there was his lucky marble. The marble reminded him of the fishbowl in his bedroom, and thinking of the fishbowl reminded him again of home, and how close he was to it.

He took out the marble and held it in the sunlight, looking into it at the bubbles and the swirls of glass. There seemed almost to be whole worlds in there. The little frozen air bubbles were like planets spinning through space.

"A marble," said Mr. Deener all of a sudden, as if the marble had brought his mind back from wherever it had strayed.

"A lucky marble," said Danny. "We got them from the curiosity shop in the Plaza."

"The Plaza?" said Mr. Deener. Then he squinted and looked off across the meadow, as if he half recognized the Plaza as a place he had visited years and years ago, but had almost forgotten. "Let's have a look."

John gave him the marble, and Mr. Deener peered inside it. "*Very* good glass," he said. "Highest quality, really. You boys have collected some first rate specimens. I used to have a marble very much like this, almost identical. Take a look at this." Mr. Deener took a marble out of *his* pocket. Mr. Deener's was almost clear, with a spiral of rainbow-coloured glass threads winding through it. It sat in his hand next to John's, with its little Christmas spirals of green and red.

"Mr. Deener loves marbles," Polly said. "He says they've got more magic in them than any other sort of glass except a church window. Don't you, Mr. Deener?"

"Why, yes," Mr. Deener said. There was something about the mention of magic that seemed to bother him, though, and he didn't say any more.

"I had quite a collection once," Mr. Deener said. "I kept them in jars on a shelf—dozens of jars, all sorted as to colour and size."

Mrs. Barlow winked at John and Danny. "Now he's reduced to keeping broken glass, isn't he?" She shook her

171

head as if it made her sad. "Throw all that broken glass out, Deener. That's my advice. Go back to marbles. They're so nicely round, marbles are. You're lucky you kept that one. That's my opinion."

"I wish I could see your marble collection, Mr. Deener," said Polly who had been silent up until then.

Mr. Deener nodded. "I'd like that," he said. "But . . . alas, that was in another country, to which I can never return." He put his hand over his eyes and shook his head, as if he were acting in a stage play.

"Don't go alassing us, Deener," said Mrs. Barlow. "We're here to put an end to that nonsense. Eat your doughnut. We can all of us go home again, once we know where home is."

"You can have a look at *our* marbles," John said to Polly. "All of you can. They're right in through the window, sitting on the dresser, plain as day."

"What a grand idea," said Aunty Flo. "Polly can look first."

So they gave Polly the glasses, and she climbed up onto the branches in order to see in through the window.

"What a lovely lot of books," she said. "Are those all G. Smithers on the shelf above the beds?"

"Forty-two of them," said Danny. "We don't have them all, but someday we will."

"And look at the pictures on the walls! I can't quite make them out."

"Those are all from *The Wind in the Willows*," John said.

"What a wonderful room." Polly peered around the edge of the window just a little. "There they are. That fishbowl must hold two hundred marbles. They must have cost you a lot."

"A penny," Danny said.

She stepped down, took off the spectacles, and said, "Mr. Deener, you've got to take a look. It must be the sunlight shining in through the window or something. The marbles are almost glowing. I'm sure they aren't common marbles. They're right in your line."

"There's nothing common about any marble," Mr. Deener said, just a little proudly. But then he pretended to dust a spot of dirt off his pants, as if that was more

172

important than looking at the marbles in the fishbowl. He very clearly didn't want to look through the window at all, and when Polly reached the glasses out to him, he stepped backward and trod on Mrs. Barlow's toe.

"Ouch!" she cried. "Keep off my foot, you big ox." She acted mad about it. "Tell them why you won't look through the window, Deener. They've come all this way to get you to take a little peek. Explain yourself." She held onto his arm all the while, pretending that she was keeping him from stepping on her toes again, but it looked to John as if she *wanted* to hold onto his arm, to steady him, maybe.

Mr. Deener didn't say anything, so John said, "Is it because it used to be your room?"

Mr. Deener nodded, but he still didn't say anything.

"You'd love what it looks like now," said Polly. "It reminds me of you, of what you'd like."

"Oh, take a look, Deener, for heaven's sake." Mrs. Barlow pulled on his arm. "Take a little bitty look. It won't bite. Here's a nice glazey for you." She took out another doughnut and waved it in his face. It smelled wonderfully fresh and hot, and Mr. Deener's eyes lit up at the sight of it.

"Maybe just one more," he said.

"Come along, then." Mrs. Barlow towed him toward the window.

John took the glasses from Polly and slid them onto Mr. Deener's face, taking care not to poke him in the eye. Mr. Deener smashed his eyes shut and let himself be led along, not paying any attention now to doughnuts. Then, when he was square in front of the window, Mrs. Barlow shouted, "Look out, Deener!" and gave him an awful poke in the back.

He stumbled forward, opening his eyes so that he wouldn't tumble over the pile of branches. He grabbed the bottom of the hanging window and very nearly put his nose against the glass before he caught himself. The sleeping Mr. Deener moaned fearfully and half sat up. "What!" he shouted. "No!"

Mr. Deener looked around slowly and fearfully at the room beyond the window, as if it were a dark well with something awful living in the bottom. In a moment he smiled, though, having caught sight of the fishbowl.

"My," he said. "Those *are* nice." Then his eyes narrowed. "What happened to the curtain over the closet door?" he asked.

"Don't know," said John. "Was there a curtain over the closet door once? Now there's a door. As far as we know there's always been a door."

"That's right," said Danny.

"And all the woodwork," Mr. Deener said, "someone's gone and taken all the paint off it. And the carpet's gone, too. I suppose it was old and had to be thrown away. I rather like the wood floor, though. Except that it's a bit of a mess, isn't it?"

"Always," said Danny. "We like to keep it that way."

"And what's this—shelves around the walls with books on them and stuffed animals. Very cozy, this room. I'm entirely satisfied with it. Are there so many changes in the rest of the house?"

"I suppose there are," John said, remembering how strange Mr. Deener's house of memories looked out there on the bluffs.

"Everything changes, Deener." Mrs. Barlow said this, standing just behind him. She talked into his ear, like a henny-penny man. "It's a brand new day."

Mr. Deener didn't answer. He still stared in through the window, wearing the spectacles. He seemed to be looking for something—for the ghost of his wife, maybe, or for his old easy-chair. Then, through the crack beneath the window came the smell of cinammon and apples, of pies baking in the oven. It seemed almost to knock Mr. Deener over backward. He reeled away from the window, back onto the grass of the meadow.

He turned around, as if to say something to Mrs. Barlow, and there lay his magical, sleeping half. Mr. Deener still wore the spectacles, so he could see clearly that it was only a man twisted up out of straw. He tore the spectacles off, unable to look at the straw man lying on its pallet. It wasn't himself that lay there; he could see that now. It was awful, and should never have been made. He handed the spectacles to John.

174

Aunty Flo nodded very carefully at him and smiled. She said nothing, but it seemed as if she could read his thoughts, and was waiting, holding her breath. Mrs. Barlow had a hopeful look in her eye, but she was silent, too. Polly took one of Mr. Deener's hands and held it, although he didn't seem to know that she had. He reached into his pocket with his free hand and drew out his marble again, and John's with it.

"Might I . . ." he started to say, but then stopped. He tried again. "Might I borrow that marble of yours, too?" he asked, looking at Danny. "You might not get it back."

"That's all right," said Danny. "It isn't the last of them, and even if it was, you could have it anyway."

"And mine, too," John said. "Do whatever you want with it." He knew he might never see another one like it, but that didn't matter now.

Mr. Deener held the three marbles in his hand. "One last little bit of glass magic," he said, "before I give it up for good." He moved his hand so that the marbles settled just so in his palm, and then he held them out in the light of the sun and the moon.

John wore the spectacles now. He wanted to see the magic work. The marbles seemed to dance and shiver in Mr. Deener's hand. Light swirled through and among them, and the sleeping Mr. Deener grew restless and pale and thin, as the goblins had just before they were gone. The straw that he was built of shook in the breeze, and the twine that clumped the straw in his wrists and ankles loosened and fell away. Slowly, the magical Mr. Deener lost his human shape, so that finally there was nothing left on the pallet but a pile of straw stuffed awkwardly into a suit of clothes.

The real Mr. Deener fell forward onto the grass. The marbles were gone from his hand.

He sat up abruptly, though. A look of pain crossed his face, but it was replaced by a look of determination. Mrs. Barlow hurried to him and helped him up. "Good old Deener," she said, and kissed him on the cheek again.

He blushed, red as a cabbage again, but this time with happiness. And when he stood up he seemed taller than he

175

had been, if that were possible, and his eyes were brighter and clearer. He turned to John and Danny and said, "I seem to be always asking you boys for a favour. I wonder if I might ask for one more."

"Sure," said Danny.

"The use of those spectacles one more time, and the use of your window, too." Then he turned to Mrs. Barlow and said very gallantly. "It would make me a happy man at last if you would accompany me, my dear."

"Well," she said, "I say. A happy man, is it? Well." She grinned around at all of them and then added, "How on earth am I to fit through the window?"

"We'll help," said John happily, "won't we Danny?" And with that John climbed straight up onto the branches, slid his hands underneath the window, and shoved it open.

He heard his mother calling from the kitchen, and he shouted, "Be right there!" It was maybe the happiest thing he had ever heard. "Hurry," he said to Danny, and boosted himself over the sill, tumbling in onto the wooden floor. He jumped up and handed the spectacles out the window. His mother was coming along across the living room, toward the hallway that led to the bedroom.

"John," she said, "have you seen my Christmas pin? The green wreath with holly berries? Oh, wait. Here it is. I've found it in my pocket. Now isn't that strange . . ."

Just then Mrs. Barlow appeared in the window. She *was* awfully fat. John grabbed onto her arms and pulled, and she popped in through the window with a great lot of pushing and laughing from below. "Oomph," she said, hauling herself into the room. Her basket full of doughnuts flew in after her.

"What on earth?" came the voice of John's mother. There she stood in the hallway along with their father. Their mouths were open and their eyes goggled, so that they looked like deepwater fish.

"Having some friends in," John said.

Mrs. Barlow stood up, smoothing her clothes. "Pleased to meet you, I'm sure," she said, taking off the spectacles and handing them out the window.

Then Ahab came through, wearing the spectacles and

with his tongue hanging out. They had picked him up from below, so that to those in the bedroom he looked as if he were swimming thrugh the air. John shrugged at his parents, as if he couldn't explain any of this, and he took the spectacles from Ahab and shoved them back outside.

Mr. Deener appeared in the window then, wearing the spectacles himself and leaning in across the sill. He tilted across it, kicking his feet. "Terribly sorry," he said, probably to the mother and father. "Door won't work in this case." And he too fell into the room in a heap, and then stood up, shoving the spectacles through the open window.

"Mr. Deener," he said, by way of introduction, and he put his hand out. "Artemis Deener." John's father shook it.

"Artemis Deener?" John's mother said. "Didn't you used to . . . Didn't we buy . . ."

"That's entirely correct. I've come back to have a look around, if that's all right. Whoops! Here comes the lad." And sure enough, Danny crawled in through the window next. But when he stood up and pushed the glasses through the window, no one took them.

"Here they are," Danny shouted through the window. But there was nothing. He looked out, and there was the front porch—the wisteria vine, the white rose, Penny the cat.

"What?" said John. "Where's Polly?" He took the spectacles and put them on, and there stood Aunty Flo and Polly, very far away now. It was as if John were looking at the meadow again through the wrong end of a telescope. They waved at him. "Wait!" he shouted.

"Let me see again," said Danny, and he took the spectacles and had one last long look. He waved back at them. "Goodbye," he said softly.

When John got the spectacles one last time, he could see that far in the distance the sleeping hills were green now and speckled with wildflowers. The big river flowed with water, like a blue ribbon out of the misty mountains. And far away rose what looked like chimney smoke from unseen farmhouses that had just awakened out of a winter's nap. Polly and Aunty Flo were gone.

177

"Who is it?" asked their mother, stepping over to the window.

"Some friends of ours," Danny said.

She looked out past John, but of course saw no one—only old Penny, curled up asleep.

John started to take off the glasses in order to hand them to her, so that she could see too. But it was too late. There was too much cloudiness, as if his eyelashes had got in the way. For a moment it looked like waving grass and distant trees and the smokey line of cloud-drift in a green sky. But when he blinked and the cloudines cleared away, there was the front porch, as ever, and the sleeping cat.

The spectacles were just spectacles now, and he put them into the fishbowl, where they belonged.

That night it rained. It was a comfortable thing—lying in their own beds and listening to rainwater running in the gutters and splashing in puddles in the flowerbeds. The harder it rained, the more comfortable their beds seemed. They dreamed about Aunty Flo and Polly and about the big house on the hill. Both of them had the same sorts of dreams—that the sleeping land had awakened, and that off in the hills above the house there were towns and villages waking up. There were people going about their business again, yawning and stretching and feeling as if they had been asleep for an awfully long time.

In the morning John and Daniel dressed warmly and put on rain jackets and boots. They were going to walk to school even though it was still raining. As they were going out, they looked once more at the spectacles in the fishbowl. "Let's take them along," John said. He wasn't sure why—it just seemed like a good idea. Who knew what would happen?

Danny nodded. "Good," he said. "Don't lose the lens, though."

"Of course not," John replied. "Here, you carry them if you're worried about it."

"I didn't say I was worried," Danny said, but he took the

spectacles anyway, and put them under his raincoat, in his shirt pocket. "I wish we had enough time to go down to Dick's Doughnuts."

"Why," John asked, "we've already eaten breakfast."

"I was thinking that we could get a glazed doughnut for Harvey Chickel, maybe."

John nodded. "We'll do it after school," he said. "We'll bring it over to him."

Away they walked through the rain. They waved goodbye to their father, who stood on the front porch. "Stay out of puddles!" he yelled, reminding them that there were plenty of good puddles lying about.

They stopped at Mrs. Owlswick's house and rang the bell. Kimberly came out to walk with them.

"Polly!" John said when he saw her.

"Who?" she asked.

Both John and Danny looked at her for a moment. John tried to remember exactly what Polly had looked like, but somehow it was Kimberly's face that he saw in his mind. This time there was nothing frightening about the confusion. He liked it just fine.

Mrs. Owlswick came to the door and said, "Try to keep dry."

John looked at Danny and Danny looked at John and Danny nodded his head, as if to say, "Yes, you're right." He didn't really say anything, though, because it didn't matter anyway. It was being home that mattered, and if Aunty Flo and Mrs. Owlswick somehow seemed to be one and the same person, well that was just fine, too.

Around the corner they went, onto Maple Street. They passed old Mrs. Jimson, the lady who lived on Grand Street, and who had been asleep for so long. She wasn't sleeping any more. She waved at them as she walked along beneath her umbrella. The rain fell harder. Lightning cracked in the distance. They hurried along. Someone else was coming toward them, from far down the sidewalk.

It seemed as if they knew him, although he was so far away as to be very tiny. He was coming along in a leisurely way, carrying an umbrella, and yet even though he was walking slowly, enjoying the rain, he was suddenly very

179

close, moving with the magical swiftness of a goblin fire.

It was the little man from the curiosity shop—Aiken Drum, if that was really his name. He had his bundle of sticks slung across his back.

John gave him the spectacles when he got up to them, and he gave John and Danny a book. It was a G. Smithers book, number forty-three. And although it looked very old and dusty, as if it had been sitting on the shelf in a curiosity shop for fifty years, it was entitled *The Magic Spectacles*, and it was the story of how John and Danny rescued Mr. Deener from himself and woke up the sleeping land.

It was all there—the whole story, just as it had happened.

"I think I've read that one," Kimberly said, "but I can't remember when."

Danny tucked the book under his raincoat, and Aiken Drum put on the spectacles and tramped away slowly down the sidewalk. In the blink of an eye he was a block away, then two, and still he walked along slowly, as if he had no real destination, but was just out walking for the joy of it. Then, blink, he was just a tiny figure in the grey distance, and the rain began to pour so that John and Danny and Kimberly ran all the way to school, and just barely made it before the last bell.

There's only one little bit more that the G. Smithers book had in it that you haven't heard yet. That book ended by telling how Mr. Deener and Mrs. Barlow married each other, and moved into a little white house near the library, on Center Street, and opened a doughnut shop where the curiosity shop had been. Mr. Deener went into the business of making marbles in the back of the doughnut shop, and soon came to make marbles that were so beautiful that each one seemed to have a bit of glass magic in it.

He gave Kimberly her own fishbowl full of Deener marbles, and then made a red and green Christmas marble for John and a pink and blue Easter marble for Danny. Finally he made a big white marble with the face of Aiken Drum in it. But you can only see the face in the light of the full moon, which mystifies everyone. He gave it to John and Danny's parents, who love that sort of mystery, and they keep the moon marble on a little wooden ring on the top of their piano.